TELI
TALES
Totally Amazing Little Exciting Stories

From South West England
Vol II

Edited by Lynsey Hawkins

Disclaimer

Young Writers has maintained every effort
to publish stories that will not cause offence.

Any stories, events or activities relating to individuals
should be read as fictional pieces and not construed
as real-life character portrayal.

 Young**Writers**

First published in Great Britain in 2006 by:
Young Writers
Remus House
Coltsfoot Drive
Peterborough
PE2 9JX
Telephone: 01733 890066
Website: www.youngwriters.co.uk

SB ISBN 1 84602 668 7

Foreword

Young Writers was established in 1991 and has been passionately devoted to the promotion of reading and writing in children and young adults ever since. The quest continues today. *Young Writers* remains as committed to engendering the fostering of burgeoning poetic and literary talent as ever.

This year, *Young Writers* are happy to present a dynamic and entertaining new selection of the best creative writing from a talented and diverse cross-section of some of the most accomplished secondary school writers around. Entrants were presented with four inspirational and challenging themes.

'Myths And Legends' gave pupils the opportunity to adapt long-established tales from mythology (whether Greek, Roman, Arthurian or more conventional eg The Loch Ness monster) to their own style.

'A Day In The Life Of ...' offered pupils the chance to depict twenty-four hours in the lives of literally anyone they could imagine. A hugely imaginative wealth of entries were received encompassing days in the lives of everyone from the top media celebrities to historical figures like Henry VIII or a typical soldier from the First World War.

Finally 'Short Stories', in contrast, offered no limit other than the author's own imagination! 'Ghost Stories' challenged pupils to write an old-fashioned ghost story, relying on suspense, tension and terror rather than using violence and gore.

Telling T.A.L.E.S. From South West England Vol II is ultimately a collection we feel sure you will love, featuring as it does the work of the best young authors writing today.

Contents

Andy Barnes (14)	69
Seth Tapsfield (14)	70
Hannah Eyre (14)	71
Lucy Harper (12)	72
Fiona Murray (12)	73
Molly Hart (12)	74
Joe Simons (11)	75
Hannah Park (13)	76
Alex Parry (11)	77
Harry McAlister (12)	78
James Timms (11)	79
Frankie Stratton (14)	80
Natasha Duff (15)	81
Sam Hill (15)	82
Eloise Liddell (14)	83
Polly Tullberg (14)	84
Chloe Stevenson (14)	85
Beth Grylls (13)	86
Emma Hetherington (13)	87
Abigail Wheatcroft (13)	88
James Eatwell (14)	89
Giles Potts (14)	90
Daniel Carr (14)	91
Nell Byron (13)	92
Charlotte Wilk (13)	93
George Mackean (13)	94
Sinéad Maya (13)	95
Richard Trubody (14)	96
Grace Denmead (14)	97
Andrew Johnson (14)	98
Nathan Chalmers (14)	99
Zachary Craft (14)	100
Amy Wates (14)	101
Ed Borton (14)	102
Jack Fisher (11)	103
Benjamin Malin (15)	104
Holley Potts (15)	105
Tom Rossi (14)	106

Sir William Romney School, Tetbury

Beverley King (13)   107

The Grange School, Christchurch

Debbie-Jayne Walton (14)   108
Alex Jeffery (14)   109
Sophie Clarke (14)   110
Kay Bowring (14)   111
Luke Lockyer (14)   112
Sammy Speed (13)   113
Chloe Etheridge (14)   114
Jess Goudie (14)   115
Lucy Griffiths (14)   116
Grant Ritchie-Haydn (14)   118
Rebecca Seymour (15)   119
Adam Burtenshaw (14)   120
Rosy Conner (15)   121
Ashley Long (13)   122
Scott Butcher (13)   123
Jason Ambrose (13)   124
Jake Kneale (15)   125
Laura Dauncey (14)   126
Cameron Collins (12)   127
Sam Adams (12)   128
Liam Talbot (13)   129
Caroline Martin (12)   130
Helen Smith (12)   131
Jonathan Bakes (15)   132
Georgia-May Davis (12)   133
Sam Sprinks (12)   134
James Shannon (11)   135
Daniel Mark Walker (12)   136
Tiffany Grant (13)   137
Heather Burton (13)   138
Adam White (14)   139
William Parkinson (13)   140
Catherine Palmer (14)   142
Melanie Groves (15)   143
Sam Mills (12)   144
Jessica Barrett (12)   145
Megan Byrne (14)   146

The Creative Writing

The Confused Tale

Around the neck of Frodo was the ring, however, in his left pocket was a blue light saber. About 200 metres from the massive yellow and orange volcano where Frodo was hoping to destroy the ring, Darth Vader enthusiastically leapt out from behind a large, funny-coloured rock and tried to snatch the ring off Frodo, but he failed miserably and tripped over another smaller rock on the side. So, to cover that awkward, yet embarrassing moment, he started to annoy Frodo, by getting up and chanting, 'Frodo, I am your father, Frodo, I am your father!' So Frodo, who was clearly upset, by the expression on his face, retaliated by throwing the ring at Darth Vader.

Unfortunately, Frodo missed, but he did manage to hit a large rock in the background, resulting in a massive landslide trapping Darth Vader, but awakening Superman. Frodo threw the ring to Superman and he caught it, so, with a sigh of relief and knowing exactly what Frodo was doing with the ring, Superman flew off with it and dumped it in the roaring volcano, where it was finally melted and destroyed.

To get home, Frodo pulled out his Nokia mobile phone and called for an eagle taxi home and an ambulance for Darth Vader, but did Frodo really have a long-lost father? Suddenly, the volcano erupted and two massive …

The world went blank, as Marge decided that Homer was watching too much TV that night and Homer went to Moe's for a beer.

Matthew Kapp (13)
Beaufort Community School, Tuffley

Lamp Post Lad And Burger Boy

It was a normal day in Pleeksville, but for two boys this day was going to change their lives *forever!*

In the slums of Pleeksville, lived Chris Knight and Matt Wateridge, these two were best friends.

On 19th May 2006, the local school of both Chris and Matt had a field trip. Matt's class had a trip to the burger factory and Chris had a trip to the Lamp Post Museum.

As Chris got to the museum and entered, he felt a strange presence in the air. The strange thing about it, was that Matt felt the same presence. Chris walked past a lamp post used by the army for testing bombs. He looked closer and then *zap!* Something sent a tingle down his spine.

Matt took a bite out of the burger that was used to find a cure for smallpox. That night Matt noticed that he was getting fatter and smelt nicer. He also found sesame seeds on his arms. The following morning, Matt had turned into a half-pound 100% beef burger.

When Chris got home from the Lamp Post Museum, nothing changed, but in the morning he found he was much taller and his nose was huge. When he looked in the mirror, he noticed a light bulb for his nose and he was metal, just like a lamp post.

The next morning Matt and Chris met up and looked at each other and said, 'What happened?'

No reply from either, but Chris, who had read too many comic books said, 'We should become crime fighters. We have the look!'

Matt didn't know what to do, so he agreed.

This formed the super team of Lamp Post Lad and Burger Boy, but what they didn't know, was that their evil foes wanted them dead. This was their biggest challenge.

Charlie Tyndall (14)
Beaufort Community School, Tuffley

Chocolate Fiends!

Perfect! That's Willy Wonka! Perfect factory, perfect hair, with its perfect little flicks, perfect guests and a perfect life!

Well, that's all so-so, but the bit about the guests, that's a no-no. There was one guest who was the absolute topsy-turvy, upside-downy, version of a perfect guest. And this guest was Wilma.

Wilma was a terrible, troublesome teenager, whose mind didn't seem to process anything, except, 'There's chocolate over there, you should eat it!' However, all this chocolate eating hadn't gone to her head, but her hips, as she was a gross size.

So it was a disastrous day when she finally was taken to the factory.

The trip seemed to be going OK, until it came for Wilma to visit the chocolate river. Now, to most of Willy Wonka's guests, this was an exciting moment during the trip, but for Wilma, it was an hysterical one. The sight of all that chocolate, whirling and twirling around, sent her into a complete meltdown. She passed out, right there, straight into the flowing chocolate.

Luckily, Willy had prepared for this kind of situation, through many sessions of watching Baywatch. He immediately proceeded to rip off his clothing in a wild, yet heroic manner, only to reveal a skimpy, red swimsuit. He ran gracefully to the river's edge and then plunged into the thick, gloopy liquid.

Unfortunately, Baywatch is obviously not the best place to get advice on life saving, as Willy couldn't make it through the chocolate's torrential currents to reach Wilma. What a shame, but what a way to go!

Kristi Minchin (14)
Beaufort Community School, Tuffley

The Twisted Tale Of Nemo And Jaws

One day in the deep of the Pacific Ocean, Nemo decided to visit the local sushi bar. Little did she know her whole life would change after ordering her spicy tuna roll.

As Jaws, the waiter, turned up with Nemo's order, he was stunned by the beauty of his customer. For a brief moment, Jaws was speechless and couldn't believe his eyes. 'Here is your order, Ma'am,' he stuttered.

'Thank you,' Nemo replied.

Just as Nemo finished her meal, Jaws swam over to tell her how he felt. 'This may sound very strange coming from a complete stranger, but you're the most beautiful creature I have ever seen. I can't stand thinking I may never see you again, please can I have your number?'

Nemo didn't feel the same way, so she gave him Radio One's Flirt Divert number instead, 'Here you go,' she said with a smile.

As Nemo swam away, she realised she had made the biggest mistake of her life. No one had ever said anything so sweet and beautiful like that to her before.

As the next week passed, Nemo regretted what she had done and went back to the sushi bar to apologise. Unfortunately, Jaws had already left. 'Where did he go?' she shouted and realised she had to do something and the sooner the better.

After months of searching, Nemo found Jaws far away in the Atlantic. 'Hey there stranger!' she said. 'I'm really sorry I was so mean. Can you forgive me?'

'Of course I can,' replied Jaws, 'I would be completely insane to lose you again.'

They swam to the Mediterranean where they could start a new life together and meet lots of new fish.

Amy Brown (14)
Beaufort Community School, Tuffley

Mrs Puzzle McFee

Mrs Puzzle McFee was well known in the town, but she was never really liked, except by an inquisitive little girl called Little Miss Lee. Mrs McFee was known in the valley as a spiteful old hag and Miss Lee was considered an outcast for thinking otherwise.

One cold winter day, Little Miss Lee gained an idea whilst lying in bed. She wished to venture to the top of Coopwood Hill and try to enter Mrs McFee's house. However, she was concerned of the trip she would take by herself, so Miss Lee went to the heart of the town and tried to gather a party of people on the venture.

Regretfully, as expected, Little Miss Lee's idea was considered a ridiculous one. Embarrassment turned to bravery for Miss Lee as she marched furiously off on the path of Coopwood Hill. Miss Lee reached the Puzzle McFee mansion by nightfall. As she slowly opened the huge iron gates, a scroll came down in front of her face and I'll tell you it stated: 'If you are to enter, you must tempt your fate!'

It continued: 'Your riddle is this: until I am measured I am not known yet how you miss me when I have flown. You have a minute to answer'.

Little Miss Lee was confused for sure, but as the clock struck 12, she was filled with awe. 'Time!' she screamed and waited for more. A key dropped down, as if it were dead and a voice then said, 'Please come in and rest your head ...'

Scott Matthews (14)
Beaufort Community School, Tuffley

The Tale Of The Friendly Ghost

Charlie the ghost lived in a huge house. He lived on his own so he was very lonely. He longed for a friend.

Hannah moved into the house with her father not knowing Charlie was living there. Charlie was so happy about Hannah moving in, he could become her friend.

It was Hannah's first afternoon in the house, so she was exploring. She came across an empty room; just a bed was in it.

'Hi!' Charlie jumped from behind the bed.

'Argh!' screamed Hannah, while running away from Charlie.

'Wait! I'm not going to scare you!' Charlie yelled after her.

Hannah ran back to her room and slammed the door on Charlie, but because Charlie is a ghost, he went straight through the wall.

'I just want to be your friend,' Charlie explained, as he came through the wall.

Hannah realised that Charlie was a happy, friendly ghost with a kind and caring smile, but she was still wary of him.

'Hi, I'm Charlie,' the ghost introduced himself.

'H-H-Hi, I'm H-Hannah,' stammered Hannah.

She soon got over the fact that Charlie was a ghost and became very talkative. They talked for hours about anything and everything.

Hannah and Charlie had fallen asleep, because they had talked for so long, but when Hannah woke up in the morning, Charlie had disappeared. She searched the whole house for Charlie, but she couldn't find him. She was so upset, as she was going to have a house warming party later on that day and Charlie wouldn't be there.

The party began without Charlie, but Hannah didn't enjoy it. she really wanted him to be there. Then a handsome boy asked her to dance and she agreed. This cheered Hannah up so much, she forgot about Charlie. She and the boy got on so well, that at midnight the boy kissed Hannah.

Then something happened. The room lit up so bright, everyone was blinded by the white brightness. The boy started to change, he became see-through and could float, then he turned into the ghost.

'Charlie?' Hannah frowned. 'I thought you had gone.'

'No, I wanted to surprise you,' replied Charlie.

'You did that all right!' Hannah said, excitedly.

'Anyway Hannah, I've got to go, bye,' said Charlie, whilst waving goodbye.

'Wait, where are you going?' asked Hannah, but it was too late, Charlie had floated off into the night.

Christina Shields (14)
Beaufort Community School, Tuffley

My Life In A Day

Washing, cleaning, cooking, doing whatever the master/mistress demands, every day is pretty much the same, well, isn't every servant's day the same? You see, I work for King Henry VIII.

I'm woken up at the crack of dawn, by a very hungry Henry demanding a big feed. After feeding the entire royal household, I then go and clean several rooms of the castle. This involves making the gigantic four-poster beds. Then, after climbing a mountain, on the scale of Everest load of washing, I might get a ten minute break.

Later that afternoon, it's time to start the preparation for the massive feast that evening. This is probably the biggest job ever, because His Majesty likes a big variety of food and lots of it! He eats like a real pig, with meat being ripped off the bones by his horrible, yellow teeth. The juices gush down his chin and onto his enormous belly - *disgusting!* More washing!

Then, after all the eating, comes the worst part of my job ever: *washing up!* King Henry doesn't realise how much washing up he makes, because he thinks by letting his dogs lick the plates, they are clean, but I still have to scrub, polish and put it all away. To add to this big job, the banquet hall must also be tidied up before I can go to bed for a well-earned sleep.

So that is my life in a day, because every day is the same thing. Boring.

Leaving is not even an option; I'll end up for the chop!

Bethany Reeves (14)
Beaufort Community School, Tuffley

The Story Of Charlie Ghost

Charlie was a normal 14-year-old boy, little did he know that as soon as he was to move to Littlewood, his whole life would change.

It all began on a stormy Friday the 13th, Charlie had just moved house to Littlewood, he was bored of unpacking and was just getting in the way, so Charlie decided to have a look around his new area. On top of the hill, there was a huge, deserted mansion, surrounded by fog and Charlie, being the mischievous boy he was, had to go up there and have a look round.

When Charlie entered the mansion, the door slammed tightly behind him, but still on he went. As he made it through to the kitchen, he opened the cupboard, but unlike the front door, the cupboard closed gently, but couldn't be opened again. Again Charlie went on! On his way around, the only noises that could be heard, were giggles and whispers, but just like the front door and cupboard, it didn't bother Charlie, so still, on he went!

When Charlie reached the attic, all that was there was a big, wooden, rusty chest, so Charlie opened it and as he did so, a gust of wind brushed past him. Charlie thought of it as nothing to take any notice of.

A couple of days later, Charlie went back with a couple of friends and again they looked around the mansion, but when they got to the attic, the door slammed tightly and loudly, then a ghost-shaped figure appeared above it. The ghost then thanked Charlie for letting him out of the chest and carried on by saying how silly Charlie had been to return for a second time. Then, the ghost leapt inside Charlie and Charlie screamed with agony.

From that day on, they have never set foot inside the mansion again. And Charlie was like Jekyll and Hyde, with the ghost inside him forever, turning him from a heavenly boy, to an evil, nasty boy.

Gemma Porter (14)
Beaufort Community School, Tuffley

7th March 1966

It started off like any other day; I went to the river, had a drink, ate a fish. It all changed at around 10am, when I saw a boy frantically looking for his parrot. I casually strolled over and he nearly stood on me! Now, at this point, most would have left and I nearly did, until I saw the tears pouring out of his eyes. I then thought about leaving him to be alone, but he suddenly picked me up and started asking questions. Had I seen him? Had I heard him? Could I just magically talk?

In a way, it was his lucky day. He had just picked up the only talking cat around.

I wasn't quite sure what to do, I hadn't seen the parrot, but should I help and let my secret out? When the boy started to get angry, I thought it best to start talking. (Well, I didn't want to be thrown into the river, did I!)

'What does your parrot look like?'

The boy jumped two feet into the air, turned a shade of green and threw me at the boat. (Now, that was worse than the river!) I kind of just lay on the floor for about 30 seconds, feeling dizzy and was unexpectedly lifted into the air and asked to talk again.

'Tell me everything about the parrot and I will help you find him. What is so special about him anyway?'

'He's the only one who understands.'

With that, the boy was gone. I guess I'll just have to find him tomorrow.

Robyn Payne (14)
Beaufort Community School, Tuffley

A Day In The Life Of A Jew In Nazi Germany

Dear Diary,

Today we were forced out of our homes and made to leave all our possessions behind. People who went against the guards were shot, right in front of us, to make sure that we did what we were told. Children cried out for help as they watched their friends and family being separated like prisoners into different camps. My husband was taken as he was believed to have 'special qualities' for work.

My father and mother were taken to another room in the building. The next thing I heard was my mother screaming, then silence. I know she has gone. I'm not stupid. There is only one way out of this place and that is to be carried out in a wooden box, dead. The people around me don't believe it's possible. They think that we will only be here for a few weeks, months at most. Who are they kidding? I've heard the Germans talking about us. 'Inferior' we're called now. We no longer deserve the title of a Jew in their eyes.

I feel that many people will die here, but I stand alone. As I write this, I am shaking with cold, sat in a room that I share with ten other people, who I don't know. Can life get any worse? I don't think so. How can it? No food, no decent water, no beds. I will be surprised, if I can keep this up for a week at the most.

Rebecca Gibby (14)
Beaufort Community School, Tuffley

Chainsaw

Suddenly, the dusty room fell to darkness. A noise came from behind the door. It sounded like an old, rusty chainsaw. The door started to open ... *creak ... creak ... creak.* I could see the shadow of the figure standing in the doorway. He stepped forward. Then again. Then again.

I pinned myself to the wall. There was nowhere else to go. I shouted, *'Help! Help!'* but no one came. I was on my own.

It came closer. The breeze from the window felt like someone breathing down my neck. Shivers ran down my spine. It was cold. More than cold, freezing. I could barely stand. Forget about holding something, I couldn't even cry, I was so scared.

It's about two metres away from me. Revving its chainsaw. Was there anyone that could save me? What was I to do? I couldn't jump because I would kill myself and I couldn't run. It was coming. Its chainsaw was getting louder! It felt like my blood had sunk to my feet. I felt as cold as the Antarctic.

How long was left for me? I saw something behind this cold figure, or was it my imagination? I heard something though, like more people coming to get me. What had I done? This shadow, holding a chainsaw, was right next to me! I could tell because I got colder!

Right, this is all a nightmare. When I open my eyes, he will be gone! One ... two ... three ... right, here goes!

But nothing happened!

Danielle Bailey (13)
Beaufort Community School, Tuffley

Enemy

Why are they coming for me? What have I done to them?

I'll start from the beginning. Well, there is this popular girl in school. She's called Maritiza, but when my mum and dad split up, my mum went off with her dad and she blames me for her dad leaving.

But it wasn't just her that lost someone. I lost my mum and I still haven't got over it. Anyway, she got lots of mates to chase me around school. Right now, I'm hiding in the toilets, praying that they won't find me. I can't wait for home time; I'll feel safe in my own room.

The bell, I'm saved again! I've just got to get home now without them seeing me. My heart's pounding with fear of being caught. The coast is clear; I'll dash across the playground to the gates. Here goes.

My legs feel like jelly. I have a deep gut feeling that I'm going to get caught. I wonder if they realise what they are doing to me. What have I done to deserve this? I feel just as bad as Maritiza. I've lost my mum and my dad's falling to pieces. Why can't she see we have so much in common, rather than seeing me as an enemy?

Oh no, they've seen me! I wonder if I can make it back to the toilets?

Ouch! I've bumped into Miss Fix and knocked all her books out of her hands.

'What is going on here?'

Sara Johnson (13)
Beaufort Community School, Tuffley

Fall Of Oblivion

Oblivion … a vast wasteland of pure evil. The holding grounds for hellish demons, bent on the destruction of Cyrodiil. The Oblivion gates are doorways from Oblivion to Cyrodiil, letting the demented minions through to the tranquil lands.

It has been 50 years since the Champion of Cyrodiil forced the Daedra back to their hellish world. Closing the Oblivion gates forever. The Daedra were condemned heretics who infested the sacred lands of Cyrodiil. A once peaceful country full of amazing and wonderful landmarks. All that was changed since the jaws of Oblivion almost destroyed all of that.

Now Cyrodiil has recovered from the devastating impact, but Daedra shrines all across the land remind them of the great battle. The Imperial City is the capital of Cyrodiil, where the Champion lived. Sadly, he was the Grand Gladiator of the Arena, a gladiator type event, where he was tragically killed when he was fighting a High Elf marksman, which removed him of his title. It was a sad event, as he was the one of five people who had received the Imperial Dragon Armour from the Emperor himself.

Since the Champion has been gone, the city hasn't felt safe. There have been strange sightings of people in black robes by the Imperial City. They call themselves The Dark Brotherhood.

A month after the sightings, the same figures surrounded the Imperial City. All of the Imperial guards were put on high alert. Suddenly, the figures summoned Minotaur Lords with all Ebony armour. A new kind of evil is born.

Zak Dailly (13)
Beaufort Community School, Tuffley

The Ash Ghost

Everything started when George and Sara decided to have a sleepover with a horror theme. That's when the trouble started. George suggested the idea of the scary sleepover. He wanted to have it in the old church, by their school. He thought it was the perfect setting. So, the next night they met at the abandoned church. All of the windows were boarded up to block people out, but that didn't stop George getting in.

By the time they'd settled in and got everything ready, it was 10pm. Before they began, Sarah wanted to investigate the place first. After wandering around for a bit, they discovered a little cupboard in the wall. George opened the dusty doors. After blowing the dust out of his face, he found an elegant pot. He peered inside and found black ashes. He passed it to Sara; she opened it and screamed! The ashes were thrown into the air and they landed on the lit candles. That made a huge bang, with a gust of smoke filled the room. George and Sara didn't realise what they had just done.

A second later a manly voice roared with laughter. They screeched and saw the scary ghost. So they both ran towards the window, but it was blocked. They were trapped with no way out.

That was the last day anyone ever saw them. Rumours say the ghost still holds them prisoner in the church. What that ghost did to them, we'll never know!

Abigail Gabb (12)
Beaufort Community School, Tuffley

Short Story

The school was cold and Rose was sat on a bench in the playground, hoping that someday the one she adores will come and talk to her. The one she wants is Conrad. Conrad is a sensitive and polite boy who hangs around with his mates and the girl he loves the most, which is Mary. Mary is a popular and beautiful girl, whom Conrad loves and she fancies him. However, neither one of them has asked the other one out.

So one day, Mary went up to Conrad and asked him out. He said, 'Yes, of course,' in a casual way, so they spent the day together.

Rose had no idea about this, so she sent Annabella, her best friend, to ask him out and Mary heard this and went straight up to Rose and started arguing with her and hit her. Conrad dumped Mary straight away for being so cruel to Rose and went off.

That night Mary went to Conrad's house to apologise about that day. Conrad let her in and as she'd gone in, Rose was knocking at the door. Mary was not happy and when Rose came in she exclaimed, 'What's she doing here? You have to choose right now! Do you want her or me?'

Conrad didn't know what to say and said, 'I will tell you tomorrow.'

Tomorrow came, however, Conrad didn't. So the two girls went to his house, where they found him on his bedroom floor, dead. In his hand was a note of love.

Laura Henderson (13)
Beaufort Community School, Tuffley

General Cloudy And The Poultry Platoon

War comes in many forms, a war for a reason, or a war for pleasure. An angered or controlled war. Unfortunately, we've got them all.

The name's Cloudy; Capon Cloudy. General of the East Farm Regiment. The Poultry Division. A high-ranking rooster and our only hope of survival. We are at war with Lieutenant Stallion and his goons, aka, West Farm Division 101.

The East Farm has rich, fertile soil and healthy crops with a steady income. The West Farm on the other hand, is the complete opposite and frankly, the Lieutenant is green with jealousy.

Our friends and family have endured many days of fighting. We will not stand any of it from this day forward. Yet, we carry the great burden of a death threat from my old enemy; Air Marshall Hawking. A vicious and rogue chicken hawk. Their secret weapon, he could potentially wipe out our whole division.

Threat or lie? I can only assume that the Lieutenant will maintain his standards and keep his promise. We have had numerous false alarms, mostly just crows. The scouts are out and the whole platoon has been on high alert, since news came that they were briefing him on his mission.

I'm baffled, first a threat, then nothing, it's awfully perplexing. Everyone's nerves are frayed.

The painful silence was shattered as the alarm was sounded, simultaneously everyone exploded into an abrupt state of distress, as a black gloom engulfed the base. They had kept their promise; East Farm was doomed.

James Oelmann (12)
Beaufort Community School, Tuffley

A Day In The Life Of ...

It was dark, only a small sliver of light shone through the curtains. I stood gazing at the same spot, the side of the wardrobe. How I wish someone would turn me around so I could actually see where the light actually came from. Suddenly, the room was filled with light. She had obviously opened the curtains. I heard the jingle of her skirt buckle as she walked down the hall. I was alone.

Later on that day, I heard the rumble of Harry the Hoover. He was making his usual rumbling noise, as he ate up the junk left by the kids. As he crashed through the half-shut door of the bedroom, the table I was on began to shake.

Suddenly, a warm hand grabbed my stem and picked me up. I was frightened, what was going to happen? She took off my head (lampshade) then unscrewed my brain (light bulb). It felt strange, it tickled. She picked up another brain out of her bag and screwed it in, then replaced my head and put me down ...

I was turned around. The side of my face, which had been staring at the same old side of the wardrobe, could now see the beautiful land outside the window.

Now all I wished, was to be turned around again, so I could see where the door was!

Harriet Bond (14)
Cheltenham College, Cheltenham

A Day In The Life Of A Window Sticker

The day started by me looking out of the window at the green fields where rabbits and foxes were running about. Then I spotted a squirrel running across the garden. A moan came from behind me and a squinting-eyed boy got up, walked out of the room. I was left staring out of the window. The squirrel was up against a tree, stealing nuts from the birdcage.

All of a sudden, a person ran upstairs into the bedroom and grabbed the cartridge next to me. He fired and missed, the squirrel then ran away, not knowing what had happened. He walked out again and I went back to staring out of the window. A fly shot past, being pursued by a blue tit. The fly ducked and dived, ducked and dodged, but eventually gave in and was eaten.

Everything was boring after that happened. I looked around the room, wondering if anything was going to happen, but nothing did. I watched the TV which was left on for a bit, but there was nothing on, apart from the news and some cartoons.

After two hours of just gazing out of the window, the boy's mother came in with some hot water. This only meant one thing … she was cleaning the windows. She approached me as I gripped on as hard as I could, she tugged and pulled, but I could not stand it when she got the hot water out. I peeled off and was thrown away.

George Hazell (14)
Cheltenham College, Cheltenham

A Day In The Life Of ...

I am in total darkness, until a light is turned on and a big black box is turned on and noises come from it. It displays images of people moving. The next thing that happens is a strange gushing sound, like water hitting the floor in the room behind the desk I am on.

A figure emerges from the room and heads straight to the wardrobe and opens it to cover itself in black, but part of something white can be seen in-between the black on one side at the top part.

I am picked up and put inside a little hole on the side of the black things on the side of this figure.

All the day I am lugged around, rattling around inside this hole. I hit numerous things, like round, flat things, I think they're called coins and I also hit things that are joined together on a circular thing. There are only three times when I leave this hole and those are when I am picked up and looked at, then I am put back. The second time is when I am used to talk with people or I am pressed slowly and then I am put back. The third is when I am put back on the desk, for the cycle to restart and continue to circulate.

Billy Holt (14)
Cheltenham College, Cheltenham

A Day In The Life Of ...

It was quite a light and sunny morning as the light shone through the curtains. It was 8.23am and my alarm went off. I was picked up, flipped open and had my snooze button pressed, and was chucked back onto the same wooden beside table, with the same old lamp, the same old dusty clock and the same old picture of when we went to Venice two summers ago.

Ten minutes later, I sang out the tune I always sing. Suddenly, a black shadow was hovering over me, shaped like a giant flying saucer. I was picked up and answered. It was a voice that I recognised, but just couldn't think who it was. She jumped out of bed and flung on her clothes and I was shoved in her back pocket as usual. It went all black and I couldn't see anything. I knew we were outside because my battery went cold. She was either jogging or walking very fast, I don't know where we were going, but it seemed really important.

As she was getting faster and faster, I got looser in her pocket. Suddenly, half of me was out of her pocket. I was trying to push myself back in, but I couldn't. Suddenly, I found myself lying on a patch of grass, of what seemed like a park or field.

I think I was lying there for at least two or three hours, all lonely, feeling run down, because I didn't have much battery left. Then another figure was above me. It was her, she had come back for me. I thought I had been lost forever. I was shoved back in her pocket. Well, today hasn't been the most boring day ever, quite an adventure ...

Camilla Gray (14)
Cheltenham College, Cheltenham

A Day In The Life Of A ...

The boarding school children are about to go to breakfast and walk over, pressing my body to the floor. Here they come! You'd think after five years of this, I'd be used to the pain, but I'm not. The only consolation I have, is the thought that if I had legs, I'd have no second thought about trampling every last one of those insignificant baboons, so far into the concrete below, that every last pore hole would be imprinted on it.

Apart from my daily wake up call, my day is usually quiet, but today is the day where I am treated like a king.

Here comes the one they call matron now. She picked me up, but instead of taking me to the washing machine like she usually does, she takes me to the window. Oh, dear no, stop, please! *Help! Help! She's going to murder me!*

She hangs me out of the window. OK, I must try to act cool, instead of completely humiliating myself in my dying minutes. Wait a second, what am I saying? I'm a rug, for Pete's sake, not a human being! Now she's shaking me and hitting me against the wall, as if trying to shake out the dust. 'Look, sorry to interrupt you on your murder session, but do you think you could possibly hurry up?' Hey, she's pulling me back in. It's a miracle, I'm alive!

Jamie Burness (14)
Cheltenham College, Cheltenham

A Day In The Life Of …

The first sign of movement is in the early morning as the cleaners come through the yard picking up litter. Then the kitchen staff go to prepare the food in the kitchens in the door to the right of me. Slowly the scruffy, half-asleep teenagers trickle carelessly through, occasionally glancing at me. The muffled loud chatting filters through the open door. I begin to wonder what it is like in there, but my thoughts are stopped painfully as a stern-looking teacher slaps a piece of paper and sticks a sharp pin in me.

As breakfast comes to an end and the pupils come out, they stare in awe at the picture stuck to me. I feel like gloating to the other notice boards, but then I realise I can't. The pupils go back to their houses.

First lesson begins and it is pouring with rain. Everyone runs, shouting and screaming to his or her lessons with their jackets over their heads, or several people crammed under one umbrella.

Chapel begins and all the teachers and masters are in the quad, finding all the faults or helping anyone who needs it, they day goes slowly.

At night, the lights go out and we are plunged into a cold silence, apart from the rumble of cars in the distance.

Tom Johnson (14)
Cheltenham College, Cheltenham

A Day In The Life Of ...

It's early in the morning and her phone has gone off. She can barely open her eyes. She stands up. Her hands rise up to her head. She picks up her phone, Clive, and reads her message. The corners of her mouth start to rise up and give a little giggle.

She goes downstairs to have her breakfast. I hear mumbling coming from the kitchen. Then I hear shouting. A last scream, followed by loud, thundering footsteps coming upstairs. Oh no, she's going to turn me up full blast. Well, in fact, she's got another thing coming, I am not going to let her do that, for two reasons. Number one, it hurts my voice box and number two, I had heard the whole argument and her mother is not being unreasonable at all. Call me old, but I think that getting absolutely trollied at a party with sixth formers at the age of fourteen, is not really appropriate for a young girl.

Here she comes. Yep, just as I thought, she's picking out a CD from the pile. I wonder what she's going to play; a nice bit of Mozart wouldn't go amiss, but no, as I had thought, that ghastly band Basement Jaxx. What kind of music is that? Repetitive junk. She pops in the CD and presses play.

'Why won't you work? You're just a piece of crap aren't you!'

I will not be spoken to like that, thank you very much!

Lucy Cadbury (14)
Cheltenham College, Cheltenham

A Day In The Life Of ...

Open for an hour, then closed again. On goes the relentless boredom of the same old tale, on and on. Why can't I just be binned or burnt? Why couldn't Dickens, Rowling or Tolkein have written me?

My spine is bent, my arms curved. Another cup of coffee is spilt on my face.

Then school starts and the kids come in. I'm put on the shelf and watch the newer, fancier books come out of their bags to show off their laminated covers and back. I long to go back to the rainforest.

I'm going to jump! I can make it out of the window, three ... two ... one ... *no!* I can't! What if I miss and land on the scaffolding outside and am put straight into the school library? Oh, what could be worse? More perfect books shipped in, week upon week. Oh God, why? Help! The length from the shelf to the floor is so inviting, my life should be over, I'm too old, too tired. There's nothing left for me here. Three ... two ... one ... *wait!* Now, three ... two ... one ...

My arms outstretched, I flip over from front to back, the wind passes through my pages. I hit the floor, my spine is bent. Why can't I just die? She picks me up, brushes the dirt off and puts me back on the shelf. Why? Why?

Night falls and she picks me up. Chapter four.

Dougie Gittins (14)
Cheltenham College, Cheltenham

A Day In The Life Of …

I heard the noisy tune going off and the moan from the figure in the bed. The figure then got up and moved around the corner, out of my vision. I then heard the noise of running water. The room was silent again the way it usually is and the way I like it. The figure came round the corner and swung me into the wall, I was blind. All I could see was white. I could hear the figure behind me, moving around. It then walked back out and left the room, forgetting to swing me back around, I hate it when it does this, sometimes I spend the rest of the day just staring at a white wall.

I then heard more movement above, voices and then me. The figure then returned, walked through me, picked up a big bag, turned around, slamming the object into me. A dart fell out of the board that hung on me. It then picked the dart up, walked a few paces, turned and threw the dart. It pierced my skin! He missed! What an idiot, how did he miss?

The alarm was set, the sun blazed through the window and the house was quiet again.

I heard the noise of a car on the gravel drive, then the noise of four doors slamming and the approaching footsteps. The figure walked in, threw the bag through me, slammed me shut, turned and left. The next time I saw it, was when it came in, turned the lights off and got into bed.

Eddy Mason (14)
Cheltenham College, Cheltenham

A Day In The Life Of ...

Inside a cold tomb of torment never able to escape but every so often I see the bright light from the outside world I either feel more full or empty. The hand either takes part of me away or puts another foreign object into my stomach. The fuller I get the more heavy I feel almost like I'm going to fall apart but I seem to stand strong and eventually I get less and less full sometimes in a matter of hours. But sometimes I just can't cope and I feel drowsy and all warm then I'm awoken by the smell of something sour and old eventually it is taken away.

One day I just couldn't cope I felt all warm and drowsy and I just couldn't stand the strain anymore. I awoke but I felt a slight breeze I could see the outside world, I felt warm and uncomfortable. *What is happening?* I kept on thinking to myself, *what is going to happen to me?* And then I caught a glimpse of it the new, younger model to replace me. I knew I was old but not this old, *what is going to happen to me? Where am I going to go? Where am I going to stay?* I was put into a van and taken away. When we finally arrived I was carried out and there were thousands of old-looking models like me. *What is this place, fridge heaven?*

Max Oyston (14)
Cheltenham College, Cheltenham

A Day In The Life Of An Inanimate Object

The curtain whipped back, rays of light beamed in, straight onto me.

'Wake up, darling,' a voice said through the door.

There was a low-pitched groan coming from the corner of the room. I couldn't quite see it. All I could see was the light outside the window right in front of me teasing me, staring at me, saying, 'Ha, ha, you're inside, I'm out.'

A figure suddenly appeared from the corner of the room and blocked off the light. He then took a giant step back heading to the corner of the room again letting the beam dazzle me again.

'Hey little guy, how you doing?' There was a cat stumbling towards me, again. Its paws penetrated into the corner of my soft wood leaving dents and marks in me. Then casually walking away as if nothing had happened leaving me with my wood peeling off like bad sunburn. He left me there like an injured soldier.

After the long morning of the harsh sun, its rays it had gone above the window. I was eventually in shade and cooling down, when Mum came in with all the washing. She came over, placed her hand on my drawer. I thought, *here we go again,* but no, she pulled it out gently, not putting me into acute pain. Then, to top it all, she set in some clean clothes instead of dirty, smelly, wet socks.

Laurie Thomasson (14)
Cheltenham College, Cheltenham

The Competition

Tomorrow would be my day of reckoning! As the sun set in a rose pink-tinted sky, I pondered if all the hours of relentless sweat and tears had paid off. Would I be victorious in my quest for first place or would defeat play its disastrous hand? Only time, an unbearable amount of time, would tell.

After a night of much anxiety, only falling asleep for what seemed like precious minutes, my morning of fate and apprehension arrived. The final preparations commenced. The competition had arrived. Competitors looked around quizzically, like duellists summing up an unknown foe. There was an element of fear in every man's eyes. It was every man for himself. My pulse rate quickened. Cavernous breaths were taken. Everyone was poised for the off. 'Commence!' The competition had finally begun.

Everyone hurtled into action. Full throttle, every man strived as hard as he could. All united under one banner. All wanted to win. This is what drove them forward, regardless of who they left coughing and spluttering in the thick, brown dust. After much hardship, pain and suffering, the race finally ended. No one could do anymore. The judges collaborated and delivered their verdict. Only time would reveal this much awaited announcement.

Now was that time. A nail-biting, gut-wrenching time. Looking back over the past months, I wondered if it was enough. Was I the best or had someone snatched it away from me like food from a starving man's plate? The judges stood up. Everyone tensed. The results were now set in stone. After what seemed like endless hours, the judges finally announced what I was hoping for, praying for. It was sweet music to my ears. A concoction of joy, happiness and overwhelming relief flooded through my veins. *I had won!*

James Popper (14)
Cheltenham College, Cheltenham

The Gates

I could feel the cold air rushing through my air. I could feel the heat beating down on me through the window. Suddenly, the door opened behind me. I tried to dig myself further into the corner and shielded my face, but it was no use; I couldn't hide. I felt a sweaty hand on my shoulder and I was forced up from my semi-comfort.

'We will be arriving at Auschwitz in fifteen minutes. You will exit the train in silence and separate into three lines; men, women and children. You will be searched and taken to the main camp. Any questions?' There was no expression in the guard's voice. No one dared question his instructions.

The fifteen minutes felt like years. Guards walked through the carriage and everyone stepped onto the cold concrete. The atmosphere was haunting and all the passengers sorted into lines as instructed. The woman behind me whispered to her teenage daughter behind her, before being violently pulled away. I didn't see her again.

Slowly, the line moved forwards, until it was my turn to be searched. My bag was snatched and thrown into a huge pile of battered suitcases behind the guards. Everything I was carrying was removed and then I was allowed to pass. As I walked through the gates, to the crowd of people ready to march to camp, I turned around and saw my husband and my children. I didn't dare to wave.

Once enough people were assembled, we were marched towards the camp. We arrived and people were separated depending on the feelings of the camp master. Many of the children were never taken to a cell, but that night I heard a lot of pleas and cries.

Georgie Moule (14)
Cheltenham College, Cheltenham

This Story Is Short And Meaningful

I was just shoved out like a Jew in 1941 from his lowly and innocent home.

The prefect shouted at me and I bundled out of the door in a mess of un-tucked shirts and ragged ties. I shivered and looked about myself for my friends. I was on a tightrope, shaking and staring deeply into the oblivion of pneumonia. The now retired conker tree, bare and effortless came to life and viciously beckoned me like an angry parent, howled and wailed like a naughty child and eventually gave in and fell into another creaky sleep. Frost seemed to grow from the autumn-dewed grass like sugar sprinkled on a freshly made pancake.

Soon after, the first flakes of snow fell and placidly rested upon that cold earth and angels danced in those heavenly, untouched white clouds. We huddled in bundles like string beans at the local grocers and we waddled with our hands up our sleeves like penguins in Antarctica waiting for the summer that would never come. Another black morning and I am dragged out of bed like a rag doll in the hand of a seven-year-old.

But wait, summer will always follow spring and spring will always follow winter. Everything with reappear in a different form yet still be the same thing. Does it really matter what we see on the outside? Beauty is in us whether we be old, young, look attractive or perhaps not. That cycle will always come round and hope should be contained in all of us no matter who we are. Penguins or not.

Holly Chipman (14)
Cheltenham College, Cheltenham

Airbus 3200

I had never liked planes. In fact, I had never liked anything to do with flying and now, guess where I was? Stood at the entrance to the new Airbus 3200. This was supposed to be the only plane that was indestructible. It was fitted with all sorts of gadgets, like internal and external engines and extra wings, to keep it airborne under any circumstances. That was the only reason I even considered it. Well, that was the worst mistake of my life.

At first, the flight went well and we took off and were cruising towards India and were passing over some vaguely inhabited islands, when suddenly, I felt the urge to go to the toilet. As I walked towards the facilities, I saw a mysterious man, who was walking confidently towards the cabin. I took little notice of him, until he walked directly into the cabin. I started to sense something was amiss, but by now the urge for the toilet had escalated to need so I decided to continue. As soon as I had sat down, the overhead announcers said in a crackly voice that the plane had been hijacked and that no one should move. The mysterious man had managed to bypass security with a knife, because, whilst a hired accomplice made a distraction at security, screaming he had a bomb, the hijacker had slipped through.

The plane was now slowly spiralling down. The emergency systems had been shut down by the hijacker, who had ripped everything in the cabin to pieces.

The sick thing is, that crash wasn't even in the news, but the important things, like Wayne Rooney's foot, oh, they were.

Peter Sullivan (13)
Cheltenham College, Cheltenham

The Big House

Suddenly, the wind dropped and therefore so did the kite. It dropped right into the garden of the 'big house'. That was how they knew it, for even David could not remember the owner. He and his four children had moved away long ago. The kids all wished that they were still there, for they got awfully bored over the summer holidays with only themselves for company.

When they reached the wall, David helped the other two over, before climbing over himself and they followed the string over to the back of a shed. They had retrieved the kite and were just about to leave, when Katie spotted a trapdoor in the very far corner of the big garden. They all ran over to it and David wrenched it open. They were looking down at a set of stairs that seemed to go a long way down.

They followed them for quite some time, before they started to widen and the stones seemed wet. As they came to the beach, for that was where the passageway led, they spotted about a dozen old chests. The first they opened, contained what looked like Victorian clothes and Mike and Katie amused themselves by dressing up, while David looked through the others. The ones without locks on, all contained normal household items, such as pots and pans and more clothes, but when he broke the rusty lock off one, the room glowed with the shine of the gold cups and treasures that filled it.

Alex Jeffcutt (13)
Cheltenham College, Cheltenham

The Fear In Cobbled Streets Through A Child's Eyes

It was Brussels, Belgium, 1939. It was a spectacular day. The birds were singing and there was not a cloud in the sky, but the dreaded war was imminent and when it came, if, through the waiting, it did come, the Belgians would not have the firepower to stop the Nazi swine, but it was going to come. Stefan just hoped it would be like the first time, that a piece of paper would save them again and the English would come. But it did come, in great force. Spectacular really.

It was then Pierre hurtled past on his little red bicycle, with a baguette under one arm, screaming something in a frightened and hurried voice.

'They're 'ere! They're 'ere!' he yelled. 'Thousands, no, no, millions! They're 'ere! They're 'ere ... !'

He faded away as he hurtled down the cobbled streets. Soon the others came. A mob of frightened Belgians hurtling through the narrow lanes and streets, like a wild stampede. My father knew why. Soon after the mob had dispersed, my father saw the living devils they called the Nazis, although, they did not bear red or have horns. They wore blue coats.

Mitchell Barwick (13)
Cheltenham College, Cheltenham

Jenny's Room

She was waiting in the bedroom, in the dark. She couldn't go to the light switch even though that was the only thing that would make it go away. So she sat there, on top of the bed.

It had been haunting her ever since they had moved to the house ten years ago. Her parents would not believe her, they just thought that it was a child's mind running riot, but it wasn't. This was for real and this time it was going to get her.

She could see it, next to her wardrobe. One false move and it would come out to get her. She knew this would be the end, so she just sat there. Her mind drifted back to her old house and how she had even been born there, but that was fifteen years ago. She knew that it would never be the same, even if they went back there, because of her new sister, Lauren.

Jenny was the light of her parents' eyes until Lauren came along and then it was the baby this and the baby that.

Why was she thinking about happiness even though she was surrounded by death and gloom and with the thing standing, looking at her? It moved like clockwork, like it was made like a clock. *I wonder how its mother gave birth?* she thought to herself.

Suddenly, like a dream, her parents came in and turned on the light, but the thing turned and then …

Christian Jenkins (14)
Cheltenham College, Cheltenham

The Creation Of A Postage Stamp

The colours, flying in. The moment of my birth, the machine assaulting my torso. Suddenly, I'm emblazoned with the head of a monarch. I'm so proud to represent authority, to be worth something. But my euphoria is short-lived. In my elated state, the dangers ahead have evaded my attention. I look round at the last minute, but it's too late. The conveyor belt, menacing, unstoppable, carries me ever closer to the inevitable doom ahead. All I see from here, is the end of the belt, like an unfinished bridge, a simple drop, but instinct tells me, that in the mouth of the great chasm below, lies a pathway, inclined as such, that a creature with no limbs like myself, can only go one way. Down.

It is, in short, a chute. I can't stand to look any longer and although I can't move my printed head, I am able to shift my gaze over to the other side of my peripheral vision. I see behind me my brothers and sisters, soul-bound by their nature. I try to warn them of the fate that awaits them, hoping vainly that although I can't save myself, I can save one of them, but alas, I am lacking the powers of dialect. My mouth bound shut, without a tongue, I am mute. Exasperated and desperate at my helplessness, I turn my gaze back to the path ahead and as I do so, I feel my side slipping away from me.

Here we go!

Joe Lamb (14)
Cheltenham College, Cheltenham

The Last Jump

The adrenaline was rushing through my body, my stomach was churning, filled with knots. The heaviness on my back was weighing me down, as I was only young then.

I kept on trying to daydream and think of something else, but every time I looked down, I was reminded of what awaited me.

I stuck my head out of the open door and my commander shouted at me to jump. It took me quite a while to register what he had said and before I knew it, I was falling through the air.

The wind stung my eyes and it was pushing up against my chin. The air was crisp and cold and occasionally left droplets of water on my face.

I was filled with excitement and shock at the same time, but I knew that I would want to do it again. My breathing steadied from its beating pace and I tugged on the rope.

As I landed, I was greeted by my squad with a pat on the back or a slap over the head. This was the first time I had ever wanted anything in my life before, so parachuting became part of my life from then. This was the first time I wanted to be in the SAS and my dreams took me from there.

This all seemed like yesterday, but here I am now, sailing through the air, plummeting to my death, fifteen years on as an SAS Commander.

Freya Meynell (13)
Cheltenham College, Cheltenham

A Hero's Last Breath

How was he going to tell his family? He was not old - in fact, he was 45, but that didn't change the fact that he had only two weeks to live.

Lung cancer was slowly killing him, in the foggy, suffocating way that it does. He kept fit. He had been a loyal friend and a faithful husband. All he did was smoke a few cigarettes each day.

He had taken up smoking during the war. They all had. His friends, his brothers in arms, had all witnessed the sick reality of war and realised that they would die. All of them. It didn't matter how, but they knew it would happen. Smoking was the only escape in those trenches.

Alex Blades had received a medal after the war. He had dragged five unconscious men to safety after a nearby tank had blown up near them and the bits of shrapnel had buried themselves in his chest - but he'd struggled on and survived the war.

He walked slowly up to the front door of his house. He opened it and the smell of his wife's delicious cooking wafted to his nostrils. The woman herself stood in the hall, wearing an apron. He sighed. He loved Caroline, but how would she take the news?

So he told her. He had been diagnosed with lung cancer. He was going to die soon - but before he did, he wanted her to know that he loved her. Her beautiful face crumpled and they stood there, sharing the pain - the end of hope?

Richard Cocks (13)
Cheltenham College, Cheltenham

Untitled

I wasn't really concentrating when it happened. I was just skipping along the pavement, when there was a sudden, short sound. I whipped round and to my utter horror, I was faced with the most heart-stopping sight; a motorbike had rammed itself into the back of a Ford Escort. Blood splattered the dark street. I could just about make out three very still bodies in the red car. As for the biker, I could see he had been plunged into the roadside ditch, head first.

A nearby woman immediately dialled 999. She told me not to go near, but I was drawn forward in horror. As I crept nearer and nearer to the vehicle, I saw the boys, both about my age and a man at the wheel. They all lay stock-still in awkward positions, in a sea of blood and glass, splashed in all directions.

I gazed into the cold, pale face of one of the boys and I swear I saw him wink at me. I rubbed my eyes, but was shoved aside to let the paramedics inspect the red massacre.

Moments later, all three bodies were being slipped into 'dead bags'. I couldn't believe I had just witnessed some people lose their lives.

'Unfortunately, all those involved were killed.'

'Gosh! That is such a shame!'

I overheard two women chatting. But the boy couldn't have died; he'd winked at me …

Minna Peake (14)
Cheltenham College, Cheltenham

A Day At School

It all started when we moved from Birmingham to Manchester, because of Mum's work. I joined a new school, had to make new friends and that is where it all went wrong. The other children here were different, or maybe I was different from all of them. They all had different interests. All they were interested in was rock music and skateboards, not football, so even from the start, I was an outsider.

Each night, I think of what the next day will bring, then I think of them. They are always there, waiting for me, lurking in the shadows. I dread to think of what they will do to me and each time I follow the crowd in through the school gates, I find out. Some days it's punching, others it's kicking. Sometimes all they want is my lunch money, those days are good days.

Lessons come and go in a haze of tiredness and dreariness. Lunchtimes are spent alone and home time is the worst. They follow me out of the school gates, along the pavement, down the alleys. I look back and they are gone, I turn around and they are there, in my face. Then their arms raise and lower in my stomach, a leg clashes with my own and I fall. I hit the ground, hard.

They do all this to me because I am different. Because I am white.

Toby Fairclough (13)
Cheltenham College, Cheltenham

By Chance

Where was I? What was I doing here?

The bolt latched across the heavy door. My fear swelled up. The dark room was the place of nightmares. I turned to four doors with an image. I was trapped. I became used to the light. I walked into the centre of the room, the images became clear. A question mark, a clock and a chequer board. To my horror, the last was a snake. A shiver crawled down my spine. I hated snakes. I had no idea how to get out, what each one meant, one was the right way out. I only had five minutes to work it out.

I worked through each door systematically. The question mark could be either. I did not know what the clock or chequer board meant. I was not prepared to go near the snake. I opened the chequer board door and was greeted with a wall saying, 'Check mate'. I opened the clock door, a message said, 'Even a broken clock is right twice a day'. Underneath was a circle of cards and a timer in the middle. One minute to go - panic gripped me. what did it mean? Chequer board, check mate - chess. Clock, cards - clock patience. Snakes - snakes and ladders. Question mark - chance. Then it hit me. They were all games. I had to take a chance. A voice said, 'Get out of jail free.'

I sprinted out of the door, into the bright light.

Ottie Henniker-Gotley (13)
Cheltenham College, Cheltenham

It Was Him

As he ran his hand up my back, we walked through the park and stopped by an oak tree. Suddenly, we heard rustling in the bushes. 'Hello?' Hugo shouted. As I moved closer to Hugo, two men with balaclavas appeared in front of us. The taller of the men, started pushing Hugo and asked him for his money. Something was familiar about his voice. Whilst he was harassing Hugo, the other one came and grabbed my wrists. He had me in a tight hold. I was scared, but helpless.

Minutes later, I heard people coming and was relieved when the two men ran off. Hugo walked up to me, 'Are you OK?'

'I think so,' I said, as my phone beeped.

We'll get you next time ... x

'Um, Hugo?' he looked at my phone.

'Just forget about it, let's go.'

I recognised the number, but said nothing.

Later that week, I met Hugo again. 'Are you OK about last week?'

'Yeah, as you said, let's forget about it.'

We held hands and walked through town. Hugo turned to me. 'Are you sure everything's OK? You seem preoccupied?'

'Well, it's probably nothing, but I think I recognise the men from the other night.'

'Really? Who?' he asked.

As those words flowed out of his mouth, I heard a noise, which scared me to death. I stood as Hugo fell, with a bullet in his back. I looked up and saw *his* face. Shock, horror and hatred ran through me. It was *him!*

Amelia Nunn (14)
Cheltenham College, Cheltenham

Journey Of A Lifetime

I stepped onto the train, my mind tripping with anxiety, whilst my heavy feet dragged, scraping the platform. Until my adopted father came to visit me, at thirty-four years, I rarely considered my natural mother. That was when I received news, my natural mother wished to see me. My adopted parents had given me a full and happy childhood, I was unsure whether I really wanted to meet her, not wanted to risk hurting my adoptive parents, casting them off like I had a new toy to play with.

A year and two months after I heard the news, a nine-hour train journey to Devon was ahead of me. I remember every detail, even now; it was June 19th 1970, leaving behind the lonely platform in the heart of the Scottish Highlands. Having not thought of meeting her, now every time I try and distract myself from the silhouette of a mother crying, holding her newborn baby for the first and last time, whatever I focus on, draws me back to that image; tears trickling down the window, or her face ...

During that eternal journey, I had concluded that she would look like me, light-haired, blue-eyed. On arriving, I stepped off, scanned the platform, which was like a termites' nest, people rushing and crashing into each other, all pre-concerned with their route alone.

I scanned the crowds for my mirror image, nothing. So, as the rabble filtered out, leaving one lady, clutching some flowers. She was my opposite; tall, slim, pitch-black hair and eyes. Overwhelmed, I began listening to her story ...

Lucy Caines (13)
Cheltenham College, Cheltenham

The Haunted House

One day a young boy was walking to his friend's house, when someone told him to stop. The young boy ran and ran. He ran past his friend's house and came to another house. The young boy stopped and walked towards the gates.

He opened the gates and saw then ghosts coming towards him. They were family ghosts. He was scared so he ran towards the gates, but they did not open. The ghosts appeared to walk casually. The boy thought they looked scary, but friendly, so he wasn't scared anymore and some of the ghosts gave him gifts.

The ghosts gave him food and a map to get home. They said, 'Come into our haunted house, if you want.'

The boy went into the house and saw one of the baddie ghosts that planned to kill him. That ghost was black all over.

The other friendly ghost, said, 'Go out of the house, out of the gate!'

He ran out of the house towards the gate and as if by magic, this time the gate was open. When he got outside the gate, he looked at the map. It showed the forest, the road, his friend's house, his house and the haunted house. He travelled home, safely.

Ryan Hudd (13)
Fosse Way Special School, Bath

The One And Only

'Don't go!' Lottie wailed, pulling on her father's hand.

'Oh Lottie, my country needs me,' Lottie's father replied, his eyes filling with tears.

'But I need you too,' Lottie was crying so much, it was hard to understand what she was saying.

'Come on Lottie, Dad will be back soon,' said her mother, trying not to make matters worse.

'Lottie, I really must go, or I'll miss my train,' her father said, kissing her and her mother on the cheek. Lottie's father unwillingly climbed onto the train.

'Come on darling, let's make our way home,' suggested Lottie's mother, placing Lottie's hand in hers.

'OK,' she said, drying her eyes.

A week later, Lottie got a letter from her father. He said that he would write to her every week. Lottie wrote a letter back, saying she'd be waiting by the door every week. 'How long till Daddy gets home?' Lottie said curiously.

'Soon, I promise.'

As Lottie had said, she waited by the door for her father's letters. Only seven letters came, but then they stopped.

Lottie wrote a letter back saying she wouldn't forgive him for not writing to her. The next day, she got a letter saying her father had passed away. Lottie and her mother were devastated. They arranged a funeral, inviting all their friends and family. The night before Lottie wrote a speech. It said, 'I didn't understand why my father stopped writing. If I'd been patient, I wouldn't have said those horrible things. Wherever you are, father, you truly are the one and only'.

Alice Graham (12)
Hayesfield School, Bath

City Of Angels

The pavement is awkward, cracked and ruined, the face of the streets. Cold seeps and crawls over our skin cloaking us in convulsions and the traffic bathes our exhalations in neon. Dogs curl around the homeless who, in turn, huddle in and around their narcotics. We engage in marcarbly humorous, metaphysical discussions over the irony of living by the roll of life's dice.

'Walking the line,' I begin meditatively, they lift their dilated pupils, but without interest. 'You're fed this preconscribed rubbish about success, from the womb to the tomb. Success is ... economic wellbeing and a few qualifications in your back pocket, the point of life for the collective audience. As an individual, it suddenly dawns on you that the 'man' and your view of success differs incredibly and there's your problem ...' I pause and shift my outstretched legs, which are unbearably numb with cold and covered in the indentations of the ground. '... Walking the line, between their expectations and your happiness, the minority balance with ease, most scrape past; slaves to the wave and then there's ...'

'... The bums like us,' someone suggests, with bitter humour. Choking laughs reach for the silence between the stars.

'Yeah, the bums like us,' I agree, grudgingly, flicking glowing ash into the swirling gloom.

'Speak for yourself,' announces a low voice, 'I'm the Jesus of Suburbia!'

There are a few hours of life that's like a party, fuelled by cheap drugs and promiscuity, but when the party's over, all that's left is life, banging on the door like a dealer, vicious and demanding to be dealt with. We somehow know we are exactly where we belong, doing what we are supposed to be doing; going the long way round, with an air of resignation and hope that storms end as quickly and surprisingly as they begin.

Adelais Mills (14)
Hayesfield School, Bath

The Secret Key!

Invading Jess' parent's bedroom, searching through wardrobes for something to wear to the fancy dress party, Jess and Chloe came to a beautiful jewellery box. It was pink, fluffy and heart-shaped. Chloe wiped the dust off from the top. They opened it. The box contained a small silver key and a piece of paper. Jess read the piece of paper: *'I'll fit inside every slot, twist me twice and I'll unlock'*.

'I reckon this note is trying to say that this key will open any lock! Let's have a go at unlocking something.'

Before you could say 'unlock,' they had used the key in two or three different locks. 'They're all unlocked!' Chloe and Jess shouted with excitement. This was incredibly weird. Were they dreaming? How could this happen?

On Friday afternoon, two bullies boasted that they had cheated in a big test; they sneaked in at break and looked through the answers. Jess and Chloe were going to get their own back using the magic key!

They ran to the school and let themselves in. They found the right classroom, with help from their torch. It was dark and scary. They found the bullies' names on the test papers and changed some answers.

'We've done it!' Chloe proudly whispered.

'I can't believe it!' Jess giggled.

The light turned on and their teacher came through the door. 'What on earth are you two doing here?'

There was a pause.

'Oh, we just came here to get our key which we'd lost. The head teacher let us in.'

They showed the key to the teacher and smiled at each other, thinking about all the adventures that they were going to have with it.

Jessica Bartlett (12)
Hayesfield School, Bath

When Everything Went Wrong!

Dear Diary

I woke up with a start. I ran downstairs to see what all the noise was for, but I stopped and looked around and realised something was very wrong. The walls and floors were made of silver and my dog, Roxy, was made of emeralds and had sapphires for eyes.

I ran all around the house looking for my mum and dad, but I couldn't find either of them. I was starting to panic. I ran outside and the world around me was surrounded by lemonade.

I ran back and slammed the door immediately. I couldn't go outside again without a diving suit or an oxygen tank. I started searching through the cupboards. I knew it was highly unlikely for me to find one in my house, but what I had seen today, was so weird I thought anything was possible.

After a while I gave up hope and just sat in my bedroom. Suddenly, the door downstairs opened. I took my baseball bat and crept down the stairs. When I saw the thing that had opened the door, I screamed, then *whack!* I hit the monster over the head with my bat.

After five minutes the thing started to wake up. I was ready to hit it again, but I realised it was wearing my dad's work badge, then I realised it was my dad!

I can't remember what else happened, but I remember hitting my head!

Rebecca Wall (11)
Hayesfield School, Bath

Apple Tree

A toad has hopped onto the tool box again … I like toads. Mother liked toads.

I bounce my ball, remembering the past events, dreading the next. I watch it slowly grind to a halt and wish I could be like that. Bouncing up, down, down and up. It seems never-ending, unlike today.

Today it's Mother's death day … there, a full stop. I wish I could leave it at that, but as Gran says, 'A tale that has to be told, will be told.' She's leaning over me now, checking what I've written. It won't be good enough, it never is. Just like her view of Mother.

About a year ago now, we were all a family, like a complete jigsaw. Mother smiled down from the apple tree, 'Race ya, Emily!' Her voice was lost in the leaves as she jumped from the tree. She was already ahead, always was. I ran after her, knowing the outcome. A tinkle of laughter filtered from the finishing line, as I stood grinning. Mother was like a sister to me. She was back in her apple tree, swinging to and fro, 'Come on, Em, I'll help you.' She outstretched her hand and that was when it happened.

A scream fastened me in place, as Mother smashed through the branches. I remember wanting to join her, to have the thrill and excitement before the lights went out.

Gran says it's bad luck to end on an exclamation. Mother ended on one, so why can't I!

Camilla Ling (12)
Hayesfield School, Bath

Naughty, Naughty

'Stop telling tales,' Mum groaned, holding her head.

'But she got paint on my homework,' Rachel cried and stormed out of the room.

'She drew on my painting first!' Louise claimed, her eyes filling up.

It was a Saturday morning and single mum Susie, was having a stressful time. Her two children, Rachel and Louise, were arguing and Susie was getting a migraine.

'Mum, Rachel had the last of the milk,' Louise called from the kitchen.

'Pop down the shop and get some more. Take the money out of my handbag,' Susie murmured from the lounge.

'Are you coming?' Louise asked Rachel. 'I'm going to the shop.'

'No, I'm staying here to look after Mum, she looks terrible!' Rachel explained, eyeing Mum up.

'I'm fine, don't make a fuss, I'll be OK,' Mum said, lying on the sofa.

Louise grabbed her coat and headed out to the shops.

When Louise got back, Rachel was walking backwards and forwards in the hallway. 'Where were you? You were ages!' Rachel screeched.

'Sorry,' Louise replied.

'Mum's taken a turn for the worse. She has a bad headache and she has just been sick. We need to call a doctor.'

'I'm fine, it's just a bug,' they heard from the background.

Louise put the milk away and went into the living room. 'Are you sure you're OK?' she asked. 'Mum! Mum!' Louise screamed, shaking her mum. 'Rach, Mum's passed out!' she called to her sister.

'I'll get help,' Rachel replied, running to the door. She ran across the street, to Susie's friend Carla's house. 'Quick, Mum's passed out, we need help!' Rachel explained.

Carla called an ambulance and Susie was taken to hospital. Susie had a brain tumour and by telling tales to Carla, the girls saved their mum's life.

Gemma Eades (11)
Hayesfield School, Bath

A Day In Laura's Life

So, you want to know what my life is like … well, first I wake up, like any normal human would, unless they're dead, but I have to wake up at a certain time, which is 6.45am, of course. Well, I'm not going to make it to school on time, if I wake up in the evening.

The second thing I do, is get dressed in my school uniform. The school I go to is Hayesfield. The school uniform is black and has a yellow Hayesfield logo.

Time for breakfast. For breakfast I usually have Snack-a-Jacks with meat paste. You might think it sounds horrible, but trust me, it tastes lush.

I'm on the way to school now. Mum's giving me a lift because she works at my school as a cleaner. I can't wait to get to school, because then I can hang around with my best friends, Tori and Treenie. They are the best.

Here I am at school. I am really bored today. Lessons are English, maths, geography, history and last but not least, German.

I'm on my way home now. I have two brothers, Jamie and Darren. For tea we are having stew - homemade. After I've eaten tea, I do homework, then I go on MSN and talk to my friends.

9pm, time for bed. Then tomorrow I do the same thing, except for lessons, but never mind. Night xx.

Katrina Fluhrer (12)
Hayesfield School, Bath

My Cat, Kibbles

Ever since I was a baby, I had wanted a pet cat. Our family cat had died when I was two, but I still remember the glossy feel of her silk fur, running through the gaps in my fingers, her fragile bones pushing up against my hand. Her loud, crackly purr and then she was gone. Run over by a car.

I had begged my parents for a cat. They hadn't let me get one, so I settled for cuddly toys. I had a toy cat called Martha, classic fat and orange. It came with a little toy brush and a plastic food bowl. I looked after it just like a real cat, but of course, it wasn't the same.

One birthday, there was a big present, bigger than all the rest. It had holes punched into it and a huge, red ribbon. Normally, I would open the smaller presents first and save the best till last, but now I couldn't contain myself. I snatched the ribbon off and threw it aside, then tore off the wrapping paper. Underneath was a box. I wanted to be careful so that I didn't scare what was inside, so I opened the box cautiously.

Inside, peering up at me, sat a tiny silver kitten that I'd read was called a Blue. It was about the size of a sandwich and its eyes surveyed me slowly. I had prepared for this moment all my life and I picked the kitten up from the box and held it to my chest.

'Kibbles!' I laughed, my favourite cat name.

Leah Graham (12)
Hayesfield School, Bath

Beauty Of Envy

It was then when she heard it, a scratch, a scrape, like claws. Lola shifted uneasily. What on earth could that be? She stood up and looked over her shoulder at the grimy window, almost unable to see anything because of the pouring rain.

Something slipped back, quick as a shot, into the darkness. The trees and bushes outside rustled.

Lola knew that someone, or something, was hiding from her. Frozen, she turned to look at the chest on Lintindo's bed. Yes, a vague tapping from whatever was inside it and was that a voice whispering?

She took a step closer, peered into the gloom and could make out a gap in the chest and a strange mist trapped within the wood. She glimpsed a silver blade of a knife and a sharp pair of teeth around her.

Lola shivered, her fists clenched without really know what she was doing and turned to run, but it was too late, her way was barred!

A cold, dark voice spoke to her in a language she did not understand. She felt a high, chilling wind and her soul being sucked out of her. Her mind froze and her body fell limp onto the ground, soulless and empty, unmoving …

Jenny Xiao (12)
Hayesfield School, Bath

Tracing My Roots

Here I am, lying on my bed, going through my head are all the new faces of the people I met yesterday. Three days ago I would never have guessed of the series of emotionally trying events which have changed my life forever ...

I went downstairs to what I thought was going to be a normal Saturday. However, when I saw my mum's tear-stained face, I realised that something was wrong.

'Elly, sit down please love,' stammered Mum.

'OK. Is there something wrong? Another money problem?'

'I wish, honey.'

'It's more important than that, I'm afraid,' whispered Dad.

This was the first time I'd ever seen him upset. I wasn't sure that I'd like what was coming.

'There's something we need to tell you. Your mother and I found out we couldn't have children, so we decided to adopt. There was one baby we wanted, she was beautiful, big blue eyes, blonde hair and the cutest smile. We named her Elly.'

My eyes filled with tears. The room began to spin, I thought I was going to be sick. 'So ... I'm not your biological daughter? My whole life has been a lie?'

'I'm sorry love, but we loved you like you were our own.'

'So why are you telling me this now, after an eighteen-year-old lie?'

'Your birth parents have been in touch. They want to see you ...'

Nina Baldwin (11)
Hayesfield School, Bath

Out The Window

'What was that?' I opened my eyes and rolled over, my heart beating like a drum. 'Who's there?' There was no answer. 'Hello?'

I heard it again, it was like a tapping, *tap, tap, tap,* it sounded urgent.

I kicked back my covers and crawled out of bed, *tap, tap, tap,* there it was again. It came from my window, but I am three floors up!

Ever since I moved to this house two weeks ago, strange things have been happening to me.

I crept towards the window, reached out to pull back the curtain and froze. I was suddenly very afraid to open my curtains. I braced myself. I pulled the curtains, hard. They came away in my hand. There, standing on thin air was … there was nothing there!

But then I saw her. She was a young, very pale girl. Her black hair long, almost wrapped around her, along with her lace nightdress.

She stood there, staring at me, with her hands across her chest, dark against the bright white of the nightdress. She looked sorrowfully at me. Then she was gone.

Puzzled, I tried to fix my curtains. My mum would kill me if she found out I had broken them and she definitely wouldn't believe me that a girl wearing only her nightdress had tapped on my window and then vanished. I find it hard to believe myself!

Francesca Portlock (12)
Hayesfield School, Bath

The Magic Key

One day, my best friend Jess invited me round to her house for a sleepover. We had been doing our exams at school and thought it might cheer us both up. We weren't just annoyed with exams, we were also both annoyed with these two girls in our class, who always used to try and get us aggravated. They were called Alex and Megan. We tried to stay away from them, but they would always somehow manage to find us.

Anyway, Jess and I being our own usual selves got up to mischief and started to wander through her mum's wardrobe, searching for a make-up box. Eventually, we found one, right at the back of the wardrobe. 'This will do,' Jess whispered, so her mum wouldn't hear us. We opened the box to see if anything was in there and funnily enough, inside was a small, silver key and attached to it was a small note. At first we couldn't make out what it said, but I managed to finally understand it and it said. 'I'll fit into every slot, twist me twice and I'll unlock'.

For a minute we didn't understand what it meant, but then we realised it was saying that this key could fit into any door. We were extremely excited, but we both knew that we had to keep the key a secret, because we wouldn't want Jess' mum finding out.

That night, as I was sleeping at Jess', we thought we would try the key out. We had an idea. We decided that we would break into the school. 'That will be a real adventure,' I said, happily. So at midnight, we got our things together and off we went.

When we arrived at the school, Jess yet again had a brilliant idea. 'Let's be really naughty and get back at our enemies and rewrite their tests,' Jess said, sneakily.

'Good one! You're a genius!' I whispered.

So we went to the school office and opened the door with the key. Then we looked through the list of tests. We then found their tests and started to rewrite them. By the time we had finished, it was one in the morning. 'I'm exhausted,' I said.

'Me too,' replied Jess, 'OK, now let's get home before Mum realises we're gone. Give me high five, Chloe!' Jess said, with joy.

'We did it!' I said, feeling proud.

Just as we were about to leave, I saw a shadow, but Jess said I was just seeing things. Then someone jumped out and shouted, 'Got you!' we both screamed, but we had been caught …

Chloe Natrella (12)
Hayesfield School, Bath

The Top Of The Mountain I Never Saw

It was a dark winter's night. I was sat on my balcony, looking out at the most beautiful mountain ever, but in my mind, I knew I could never go to the top. Every night, I had the most amazing dream; it was about walking up to the top of the mountain, just standing there. Then I look around, that is where my dream ends. I get that every night, hoping to know what happens next, but I have never found out, I doubt I will.

It's like a book, page after page, you sit reading, but you never find out what happens next. I have been saying to myself, the end of the dream will be when I get up to the top, finding what's up there, finding the next piece of the puzzle. I have been sat out on the balcony for ages now; I had better go to bed.

The morning after, I'd had the same dream. I sat up in my bed, thinking I was on top of the mountain, but I wasn't, I was in my room, looking around. I was hoping to get the next chapter of my dream.

It was killing me, not having my wish. I just had to wait. I knew this was a dream that was going to last the rest of my life.

Now, I am 40, I have never had my dream, I will never find what is up there, I will never get to the next chapter of my dream.

Shanna Towner (14)
Hayesfield School, Bath

Flying With My Grandma

My eyes were hurting. I didn't want to open them, but I didn't want to close them either. I had never seen my grandma properly before, but now it was my real chance. I couldn't waste it. I stared at my gran. I waited for her. She didn't say anything, she just stood there, in thin air.

'Come on,' she whispered.

I was shocked. I thought I was in a dream, but I was on my bed. I could feel everything in the room, except for my grandma.

'Come on,' she whispered again.

'How are you here, Grandma? You died when I was only three-year-old.' I mumbled.

'There's no time for questions now, darling. You must come with me, sharpish,' she said.

'But Gran ...'

She interrupted by putting her finger on her lips and saying, '*Shh*, darling.'

She flew over to the window and opened it wide. I walked over to the window. The breeze was cold and calm. The moon was shining bright. Gran took hold of my hand and flew out, pulling me along too. We were out! I stared back to see my house. There was nothing there! I looked, she wasn't looking at me.

Just then I realised I was flying too. I was actually flying! Grandma looked at me and smiled. Then I knew. I knew that it wasn't just my grandma that was the ghost, it was me as well.

Ephrath Amin (12)
Hayesfield School, Bath

Norm

Shafts of moonlight fell across a bed, where a beautiful lady slept. She would never stir again. A bawling baby lay in a cot beside her. Another was in the midwife's arms.

'Sir, you have a baby girl, what will you name her?' she enquired.

'My wife and I were going to call her Elizabeth, but, seeing as she is the reason for my wife's death, I don't see the point in keeping her at all, as I have a perfect baby boy,' John replied.

'But, Sir ...'

'In actual fact, send her to Norm! Immediately!' John roared.

'But ...' the midwife spluttered, but a look from the master silenced her.

The baby was put in a carriage and sent away and was never even thought of until twelve years later.

The master's son, Edward, was seriously ill and was going to die unless a donation of blood was given to him. Trouble was, he was the only person who had his blood type.

'Sir, does your son have any siblings at all?' Dr MacCloud asked.

'Certainly not!' Edward cried.

'He does actually. His mother had twins and she died giving birth to the second one, a girl. I could already see that she bore a strong resemblance to her mother, so I sent her away,' John croaked.

'Well, just get her back and save my neck!' Edward said, a little shocked.

'It's not that easy. I sent her to Norm,' John whispered.

'Oh dear,' Dr MacCloud mumbled ...

Anna Jollans (12)
Newent Community School, Newent

Caspian

'Do you think he's dead?' asked a voice.

'I think he's asleep, give him a chance, he may wake.'

Two men stood over me, one with a ghostly white beard and flat cap, the other dark. 'Ah, here he is,' smiled the first man.

'Wha … ?'

The two men took my hand and pulled me up. 'Alright lad?'

'Let's get you to safety,' said the second.

'What about my boat?' I asked.

'We'll moor her, laddie.'

I nodded and followed the men up some stone stairs into a little, warm, stone house. The kitchen was lit by a fire.

'Take a seat, lad,' smiled the first.

'Sorry, what are your names?' I asked.

'Joshua and this is John, my father.'

I sat in a battered armchair.

'And may I ask what your name is?' asked Joshua.

'Iain Turner,' I muttered.

'Nice to meet you, Iain.'

I sat in the chair looking at pictures on the wall. They were of a boat called 'Caspian'; a beautiful canal boat, red with a long blue wave painted on one side.

I was soon tucking into John's homemade stargasey pie. I looked again at the pictures. Joshua caught me and smiled. 'Beauty isn't she!' he beamed.

I nodded.

'Still got 'er, but sadly, she looks like a pile of wood,' Joshua sniffed.

'Oh, will she ever be back on the water?' I asked.

Joshua shook his head miserably. 'She's seen the world, now she needs to see the repair man,' he chuckled.

John came over. 'She did indeed see the world,' smiled the old man.

'Asia, America, Canada, you name it, she's seen it,' said Joshua.

'But she's just a canal boat,' I muttered.

'Aye, she may be one on the outside, but on the inside, she's a ship,' chuckled John.

We all laughed.

'But let me tell you, it would be amazing to see the world outside this little old place.'

Rebecca Wilcox (12)
Oldfield School, Bath

Hunted

Dread was flowing through my body steadily. It throbbed with every pulse of my blood. I could hear them coming. They had been following for a while now, but I had always been just out of earshot. Just out of reach. Now however, their footsteps were pounding through my head, rebounding in my skull, until it ached. They were too close. I could sense them, just metres behind the uprooted tree I crouched behind. There was no choice, I would have to run for it, or forfeit being caught. I could hear their breath; could almost feel it down my neck. It was now or never.

I darted out from behind my hiding place and shot to my right, not daring to look behind me. Running through the trees, was nothing like I'd ever done on the school race track. That was even and flat. The woodland I was now coursing through, was slippery with mud, the uneven ground threatening to trip me. I hurtled round a large trunk, hoping to confuse my pursuers, but I did not see the tree root that, instead of anchoring the tree to the ground like its fellows, decided to protrude from the side of the tree at such an angle, that my foot got caught in its midst and caused me to tumble over.

It was as if the world had suddenly gone into slow mo. My body was dragged down to the sodden ground by gravity. I knew it was all over, as I lay face down in the earth. I let its muddy smell fill my nostrils as I felt the *thud, thud, thud,* of footsteps approaching.

They turned my body over and a face loomed into view. One prodded me on my shoulder and said, 'Tag! You're it!'

Chloë Gwatkin (13)
Oldfield School, Bath

Last Duchess - Last Thoughts

Why does he look at me so angrily, so suspiciously? I have no memory of doing anything wrong to hurt him - he puts me in purgatory and confuses me, like a blindfold over my eyes.

His own eyes shoot looks of venom at me, when the messenger boy brings me cherries, but they look so sweet and red, I can hardly help but smile - just that one look from my husband, brings an end to the blush in my cheek and my smile.

I am afraid now, what is he whispering to the soldier in the courtyard? Why is that soldier there, with a rifle?

He glances back up at me and pure hatred glows around his face like a grim halo. I have to turn away and in doing so, I hear distant footsteps approaching. Who could it be?

I notice that the soldier has left the courtyard, but my husband is still there, as if he's waiting for something to happen. He has the same smirk on his face, as when he has come back from a successful hunting trip with his friends; a cold, triumphant look of arrogance.

I do not know what plan he has come up with, but I sense it's not a happy one and I feel sorry for the poor soul for whom this scheme is intended.

The footsteps are coming nearer, approaching my bedroom. I can feel my heart quivering in my throat …

Tatiana Bovill-Rose (13)
Prior Park College, Bath

Finding Failure

This is the end. Tomorrow's the new. My fifth chance. Each time I have been found. More people seem to know. Six names, this is my seventh. I've started university three times. I know the curriculum off by heart. Does it show? Do they recognise me? I was a killer. I've changed during my life. I have been punished. I've learnt my lesson. Everyone deserves a second chance. I wish they could see it from my perspective.

Journalists only care about the story. They don't think whose life they are destroying. I've worried for ten years. I will never be able to stop. When I go out I have to be Emilia Johnson, not me. I dye my hair brown. People can spot the photo similarities. In London, I wear glasses or hats. So I can hide away.

I stare down at the lonely face. My heart floods with excitement. My career has begun. I buy the paper and arrange a taxi. I arrive and start my search. The street is easy to find. I stand at the door, about to explode. Questions start to fill my head. Who? Why and how? I take a deep breath and knock. An old man answers the door.

I arrive at the office. The next day has begun. The paper is thrown at me. The man on the front laughing. Emilia Jackson is found. I have failed.

Emilie Milton Stevens (14)
Prior Park College, Bath

Made To Believe

He sat opposite me with a smirk on his face. Again and again he asked for the events of the last five months. The dreaded question came again, but this time I did not know how to answer.

The next morning, Sam and I were woken up early; neither of us had said a word since yesterday. I entered the same room as before. There stood the same table in the middle with a tape recorder. I could feel all the eyes watching me through that mirror. I had been in this situation every day, since my parents had been taken into custody, but this time a different man was perched in the chair. He gestured for me to sit down opposite him, so I did.

He proceeded to ask me questions and questions. After a few hours, my eyes were red raw, my cheeks blushed from all the salted tears. Then I realised what was going to happen. We would be separated!

I can't remember the day my loving parents began to hit me. I don't remember any of it, but it must have happened. If it didn't happen, then why all the questions? I can't remember when all of this began or if it began.

The day we were brought in here, I was adamant none of it had happened, but now, after two months of gruelling questions, maybe it did happen, because that is what I'm told!

Natalie Dann (14)
Prior Park College, Bath

Run Zahir, Run

Running beside the car I was driving, was a young Indian boy, who looked no older than five. Following close behind the boy was a tall, thin man with a stopwatch swinging around his neck. Trailing the small boy and the man, were a multitude of cars and vans, mostly journalists covering the adventure of this remarkable child with a huge talent for long-distance running.

About a kilometre ahead of the group of cars, was a large crowd of cheering people. They were shouting and calling out, 'Run Zahir, you can do it!'

There was a red line daubed straight across the dusty path. As we came closer to the congregation, they started chanting his name. Two women were holding a thin, red tape across the dirty lane.

The hot sun beat down on the path, making it much harder to run. Drops of sweat rolled down Zahir's face. Despite the boiling temperatures, he carried on.

When he reached the group, the noise became deafening. Nevertheless, this did not seem to bother the young child prodigy, as he crashed through the tape.

He had just reached thirty-two miles and broken the world record. Cameras flashed all around, this moment would go down in the history books. Whilst all the chaos was going on, nobody realised that Zahir had carried on running. Not only had he just broken the world record, but he wasn't even finished yet.

Zahir stopped eight miles later.

Catriona Murray (14)
Prior Park College, Bath

Discovery

I've always loved volcanoes. That's why I came out here in the first place; I just wanted to feel the excitement of working with something so powerful, but I never expected this. It's not easy being an ex-pat, though. I knew it wouldn't be, especially at times like these.

I was working in a government lab, analyzing tremors from the past two weeks, when I noticed something very strange, something I couldn't explain. I searched the archives and database for hours, looking for a solution. I finally found an example of where this pattern had happened before, only this time it was on a bigger scale. It suddenly occurred to me, I ran through the possible outcomes once more and I was sure.

I darted up the last few steps and knocked on the door.

'Come in!' called a voice from inside.

I entered, almost crawling and put the graph on his desk. He knew what it meant, but he asked all the same.

'The volcano,' I mumbled, waiting for a response, 'it will erupt. Soon.'

He said nothing, but picked up the phone and muttered something to his secretary. There was another chair on the far side of the room, near his.

'Sit!' he ordered, pointing at the chair. 'We must wait.'

We stood as a man in a suit came in. The soldier that followed him made me aware of who this man was.

'How long do we have?' they looked at me, hoping for time.

'Seventy-two hours.'

Alexander Smith (14)
Prior Park College, Bath

My Dream

The sun was shining through the undulating waves; all was peaceful as I lay on the sand, gradually feeling the heat warming the scales on my back. The water around me was a vivid turquoise which was distilled by other fish darting about. I slowly glided through the water, stopping for an occasional bite on a rogue piece of weed that tumbled along the sand.

As the day drew on, I returned to my forest. My forest was vast; it was made up of seaweed, coral and rocks. The entrance was a small hole made up of pink and blue rocks, which the sun glinted off. The canopy was made of seaweed which hung over the coral either side. Inside, the sand was warm as the sun could seep through the canopy. I went to sleep.

I woke up, so I decided to go on a journey to the other side of the sea. I glided slowly through the water. I noticed other fish swimming by. The shiny grey tuna swimming in shoals, the pufferfish full of air. This was the life. I toiled on. I passed through the underwater volcanoes, so hot that they would fry a fish in five seconds flat. That was when I realised something was wrong. No other fish were here, it was deserted. Then I felt the material of a net stroke my back and I was being lifted, taken away.

George Hyde (14)
Prior Park College, Bath

The First

The snow, which made a pleasant sound underfoot, became yet another annoying feature on the growing list of pains and irritations, but I was comforted by the thought that I would be there soon. I was on the home straight. Luckily, it was pretty flat for the next fifty metres.

I could see it, the marker, standing tall above everything. I almost ran into it, but I knew my legs could not take it. The pole had a sign that read: *Mount Everest, The Top Of The World!*

I had done it, I was the first. Like the first person on the moon, or the first person to sail around the world. Ever since the car crash I thought I would be useless. Now look at me, I'm the first person to climb Mount Everest with prosthetic legs. I looked out into the clouds. It was like Heaven. I was above everything that ever existed.

I stood there until ice started to gather among my eyebrows. I had promised to ring my wife when I got to the top. 'Hello honey,' I said, 'guess where I am!' She broke into tears.

'Are you going back down in your wheelchair?' said one of the guides, with a smile.

I laughed, 'Maybe next year.'

Andy Barnes (14)
Prior Park College, Bath

Lost

Wandering endlessly, clueless, lost, dying.

There was nothing for me at home. I had left Angola to search for a job elsewhere. My family had been consumed by AIDS and I had left in fear of it. I left without a penny, rags for clothes and crumbs for food. I had nothing. It was then I started stealing and begging. I had always been a fast runner and throughout the last year it had been a godsend. At the start I had tried to pickpocket and without any practise, got caught many a time, however I always managed to peg it. Over time though I became expert at it. A year of this was enough to book myself a one-way ticket to America.

I arrived, no baggage or life. I was to restart here. To build a life that had been knocked down time and time again. Everything seemed to require a CV and a formal address. I had neither. Life was going to be hard, but at least here, there was no fear of disease.

I sat down under a superstore hangover, put my ripped hat on the floor and waited for any generous people to stop and give. I received about a dollar on my first day, which helped me to buy the first proper food I had had for about six months.

Next day I went to get myself a job as a street cleaner. I was still lost, but not clueless or dying.

Seth Tapsfield (14)
Prior Park College, Bath

Lifeless And Faultless

They pushed her against the wall of an old, empty warehouse. Her pale skin, red with blood. They were unemotional and unsympathetic. She cried out in pain, they pretended they could not hear her. They pulled at her long blonde hair, scratched her bloodstained skin. The cuts re-bled.

Laura always had trouble in school. She had changed schools more times than she could remember. The girls were always horrid, but never to this extreme. These bullies were in a whole different league.

Once again she let out a scream as the biggest bully punched her in the stomach. She fell to the ground, writhing in agony. Laura attempted to stand, but was shoved down once more. Circling her, one at a time kicking or throwing stones at her limp body. Now a small puddle of blood surrounded her, still they continued this torture.

The girls showed no mercy towards Laura. They just thought that she deserved it. They believed she was pretty and popular.

The truth, however, was that Laura was not popular, most people presumed that she was mean and therefore, intimidating. She only had one close friend and the bullies had left her to die, further away from this crime scene.

Laura had slowly ascended to her feet. This time they allowed her. A gaunt girl handed a piece of debris to the leader. She then took the debris and in one swing, smashed it against Laura's head. She fell. Lifeless and faultless.

Hannah Eyre (14)
Prior Park College, Bath

The Lost Pigeon

It's my birthday, a vital person is missing and he promised me something special. At last, he arrives with a basket containing four young pigeons. They're all beautiful, but one is small and pure white.

They are all very young and I will have to feed them until they're old enough to go into the pigeon house outside. They don't have all their feathers yet, but wonderful yellow beaks and pitch-black eyes.

Of course, I name them all, but Jeremy is the smallest and rather a favourite.

After five weeks, they're ready to fly. The last to leave is Jeremy and as I open my hands, he flutters to the roof. I beam with delight and happiness. A good job done.

It's wonderful seeing my four pigeons flying around the house and always returning to the loft.

Then one morning a sparrow hawk appears - I had seen him in the top field - but how do I warn my pigeons?

That evening, only three return and Jeremy is not with them. After all, he is the smallest and nature can be very cruel.

The following morning, I throw the corn as usual - suddenly, there's a rush of wings and Jeremy appears from the conifers. Clever, clever bird, he has survived!

Lucy Harper (12)
Prior Park College, Bath

The Knockout

The ball flies towards Mark and the *thwack* echoes round the field. Mark shrieks in terror as the maroon ball hurtles in the direction of his hot, red face. 'Go on Mark!' yells his agitated mother, jumping wildly by the pavilion. 'Go on Mark!' shrieks the rest of the team, staring in his direction.

A minute later, he is lying dazed on the ground. There is a crowd around him, his mum weeping on her knees beside him. An ambulance speeds into the field and the crowd disperses.

'Right, young lad, what's your name?' asks a young paramedic.

'Mark!' screams Mark's mother.

'I'm sorry, but we need to take him in.'

'Whaaatt!' wails his mum.

As they arrive at the hospital, Mark begins to come round and the worried look on his mother's face drains away.

'Uhhhhhhhhh,' he moans croakily.

'It's all right, you're in hospital,' says a kind nurse in a dark blue uniform.

'My eyes! I can't see!' says Mark.

'Don't worry, it is natural. You were knocked out.'

As the day moved swiftly on, Mark was in full swing, apart from the bruise on his forehead. His mum was back to her cheery self and Mark … well, Mark had been made Cricketer of the Year. He caught the hit he was knocked out by after all. When he fell, the ball landed on top of him after knocking him out. He returned to school the next day, to find a big, shiny brass shield on his desk.

Fiona Murray (12)
Prior Park College, Bath

The Pearl Story

A long time ago, on a hot summer's day, a ship was sailing through the warm waters of the Caribbean. A young girl was travelling on this ship with her foster parents. They were going on holiday and her parents had decided that it was the best time to tell her the true story of her life.

Her mother called her over from the side of the deck and sat her upon her knee. 'Your father and I have decided to tell you the truth about how you came into this world,' her mother said, softly.

'It started off when your Ma and I were just a young couple,' her father said. 'I brought Ma a pearl as a gift, but then something strange happened.'

'The pearl grew into a baby that was you,' her mother whispered in her ear.

That night, the girl couldn't sleep. She tossed and turned and her golden hair lay matted with sweat.

Whoosh, whoosh!

The waves seemed to be calling her, saying, 'Come play with us.'

Slowly, in a trance, she rose and climbed up on deck. The waves were still whispering. Suddenly, there was a splash and a flick of scales and a mass of golden hair and she was gone.

So, be careful if you come upon a pearl, because you never know if it will grow!

Molly Hart (12)
Prior Park College, Bath

T.A.L.E.S.

The great fortress stands in front of me. 50,000ft of wood and metal. It is a slide like nothing I've seen before. I put my foot on the first step of the ladder. Steadily, I grab on and start to climb. The ladder is brittle and wobbles from side to side. I slowly continue climbing. My entire body is trembling with fear. I think of the achievement and glory I'm about to win, to build up my confidence. I'm now climbing with speed like a squirrel up a tree. Just a few more steps to the top. Suddenly, my shoe slips on a step. My arms are holding me 50,000ft in the air and it's freaky. I pull up, straining my muscles. Nearly there! I'm safe again. I feel relieved and strong. I feel like an explorer that has just found a mummy's tomb. I feel like a pirate who's found the buried treasure. I feel special.

At the top, I can see the whole of the world. It's higher than Everest. Over the edge my family and friends are cheering. 'Slide Joe, slide!' I sit down and slowly dangle my legs over the edge of the slide. I gulp and lower myself down. *Whoosh!* I'm falling at the speed of light and my hair is swaying around. This is the greatest thrill of my life. I feel like a daredevil who's jumped out of a plane. I feel like the proudest little boy in the whole wide world!

Joe Simons (11)
Prior Park College, Bath

Fairy Circles And Pixie Woods

In Dream Wood there are six pixies and a goblin. In Silva lake there are two mermaids and a dolphin, and in the Murky Moors there is a fairy ring where three fairies live called Moon, Star and Sun.

It is the middle of the night and the pixies are dancing, the mermaids are singing and the fairies are guarding their circle.

'We have run out of berries, Moon. Can you go and get some from Dream Wood?' said Star. So Moon went to Dream Wood to get some berries.

'Star, we have run out of water, please can you go and get some fresh from Silva lake?' said Sin, so both fairies ran off to get their things.

When Moon got to Dream Wood she collected her berries and started to leave, but suddenly a pixie grabbed her and dragged her back into the wood.

When Star got to Silva lake, a mermaid grabbed her foot and pulled her in.

Sun went to look for them. When she got to Dream Wood, she saw Moon in the sky, shining like a silvery orb and when she got to Silva lake, Star was in the sky, as a twinkly dot. When Sun got back to the ring, she realised she had been hit by an arrow and she rose to the sky as a flaming hot circle.

Hannah Park (13)
Prior Park College, Bath

First Trip To The Shops

It's my first trip to the shops today. It's just across the next road, but I've never been by myself before.

Mum says to look after the money carefully, buy only what she's asked for and to certainly never get run over. I set off happily, very proud that Mum thinks that I'm big enough to go out on my own.

I wait quietly by the zebra crossing, as cars whistle by. It takes ages for the cars to stop, but they do and I walk quietly across the crossing and turn left to the shops, standing quietly in the distance, all huddled together.

I go into the Co-Op and get all of the things on Mum's list, pleased that everything has gone so well, so far. I stop at the check-out and unload my things onto the counter and fumble in my pockets for the twenty-pound note that Mum gave me to pay for the shopping. It's not there!

I leave the shop after explaining my predicament to the cashier, who is very understanding. I'm going to look for the money, retracing my steps until either I find it or I get home.

There's no sign of it anywhere. I've checked all the gutters and drains and anywhere else I can think of.

I've got home now and Mum's opened the door, expecting to see me laden with shopping, which I'm not. I tell her all about my trip and she says it was very silly to get so excited and I'd have to go and apologise. I refuse.

Alex Parry (11)
Prior Park College, Bath

The Safari

What a fantastic experience for Harry, who was on holiday with his parents and sister in Kenya. They were taking a two-day safari trip. They had to be up early for the long drive to the Tsava East Game Reserve. The roads were very bumpy and the driver drove like a lunatic, frightening Harry and his family, almost to death. Pleased to arrive safely at the game reserve, hot, dusty and tired, they found themselves bombarded by the locals who were trying to sell hats and other souvenirs. Just to get them to go away, Harry's dad bought a hat for Harry.

Travelling slowly around the game reserve, Harry and his family were unable to believe their eyes. First were the gazelles and then the monkeys, they jumped all over the vehicle pulling at the windscreen wipers and playing with the aerial. The vultures looked extremely scary, but the giraffes were so very graceful, but the most wonderful sight for Harry were the elephants. They marched along with the male at the front, followed closely by the rest of the herd, which included a baby. The day was rounded off when Harry spotted three lions just sitting in the grass. The driver said they were probably wondering what to have for lunch!

Suddenly, and without warning, they jumped up and charged at the vehicle ... the driver put his foot down and all that could be seen out of the back, was a big cloud of dust!

Harry McAlister (12)
Prior Park College, Bath

A Fairy In A Desert

I strutted through the desert. No life, no sound, no sight for miles and miles. The sun blazed like flames. I knelt down and started to crawl along the sand. The sand felt like lava. I turned and saw a small light. It moved from here to there and as it came closer, it transformed into a tall man who stood in front of me. 'You, crawling in the sand, who are you?' he shouted.

'Odewssa, son of Egeum!' I answered.

'Why are you in the desert?' the man asked.

'I was banished for stealing a loaf of bread from a baker in Sparta,' I answered.

The man turned away and turned into a yellow light, but he wasn't leaving. He twirled and swirled and then the light exploded. I was knocked out by the blast.

When I opened my eyes, I was looking upon a huge, ugly troll. It bellowed and growled. He lifted a huge hammer, which he swung, *whoosh!* It swung over my head. Next time, he swung it lower and faster, it hit my chest and I was thrown back, then there was a dazzling light and a swarm of fairies bombarded the troll. He gave a huge cry and dropped with a huge thump onto the ground.

The man walked towards me, he snarled and drew a sword. The fairies suddenly transformed into beautiful women with flowing gold dresses. One of them stepped in front of me and drew a wand. She cast a spell at him and he was thrown back.

'Why did you want to hurt him?' I questioned.

'It was because that creature wanted to kill you,' she replied.

'Why?' I asked.

'Because he is a murderer, a villain of the fairy world and a servant of Satan. He kills lonely souls.'

I gasped and ran away as fast as I could. I tripped on a rock and flew through the air, hitting a rocky boulder and dropping back, dead in the sand.

James Timms (11)
Prior Park College, Bath

Suicide Note

Dear Finder,

Whoever you are, you are reading the past, a past that can never be found again. Having no one special in my life, or no one to care for me, this letter will mean nothing to you, it means as much as my life meant to me, worthless. In fact, I don't even know why I am writing this letter.

The jealousy and loathing I felt towards those people who had loving families, who cared about their child's lives, who squeezed out every moment that life could offer. The opposite of this is what I got and it is why I felt there was no point in my life anymore. It was just a blank piece of paper. I was waking up in the mornings, dreading the pain-ridden hours of hard labour on this disgustingly inhumane piece of farmland they called home. This was no home, this was prison, it even felt like Hell itself. No matter how hard I tried, it was never good enough for you. I myself do not know how you lived your lives like this, but I will let you know it has forced me to take my own.

When you find this letter, I will be no more, this is the end for me, I can go on no longer and you have driven me to my death. If God has pity on you, I will see you in another life.

Edward.

Frankie Stratton (14)
Prior Park College, Bath

A Place To Call 'Home'

What is this place? This place that I call home? So much for that. As far as I've always understood, home is where the heart is - isn't that what they say? Well, my heart certainly isn't here. It's far, far away from here.

This must sound so clichéd, but it's true. Every evening I go to this amazing forest, across some fields from my house. I'm always there alone, just me. I'll run away from my house, I'll keep running for ages and suddenly, I find I'm in this forest. I sit and feel so at home and I can just sit alone with my thoughts and not a worry in the world.

And then one day, I ran to my forest, but when I got there, it was gone ... my forest had gone. Someone had cut all the trees down and it was gone.

I stood at the front, looking into what was now just an open space with logs all over the floor. How could this have happened? No one could possibly have taken away my wood, it was my home. You don't take away people's homes. You just don't. I felt so empty ... how could someone have done this? I just didn't understand. I stood there for hours, hoping it was all a nightmare. Reality isn't always pretty - some selfish person had ruined my dream, my home, my hopes. It was mine and it was all gone.

What is this place? This place I call home? Why can't I have it back? After all, home is where the heart is, someone's taken away my heart. I want my home back, I want my heart back ...

Natasha Duff (15)
Prior Park College, Bath

Silence Is Saffron

I feel my way towards the hospital doors, rushing my way. Confusion rife, I stumble and lunge at the reception desk and slam the bell, which splits and falls in two, the receptionist came running, still struggling for words, in a breathless stammer, I ask for directions to Ward C, room 14. She points in the direction of a small archway and I run towards it, heart pounding to the beat of my steps, counting down the rooms beside me, antiseptic overpowering my thoughts, I bustle through a large congregation of medical staff and cascade into room 14. I look upon my wife … her charm-invested face lies jaded, a nurse looks up to me, though she immediately turns to a cloudy blur, my eyes streaming.

'I'm sorry, she hasn't woken,' the little woman says.

I kneel to her side, clasping her hand tightly within mine, reaching over I run my hand through her golden hair, face strained and expressionless, rubbing my eyes on my sleeve, I turn to the nurse sitting across the room from me, perched upon a rickety chair.

'Is she going to be … ?' I whisper and then the silence, her eyes starting to glisten with tears.

'She has internal bleeding and …' she paused, looking down at her lap, 'your child has died.' Fading away towards the end and sliding out of the door. My head falls, nestling by Sarah's side, I weep, my body clenched in loss.

Waking up, I feel a tender embrace upon my hand, looking up I see a face on which I gaze upon so fondly, lost of words, I say nothing, silence became saffron …

Sam Hill (15)
Prior Park College, Bath

Short Story

I awoke. My eyes widened. Standing at the end of my bed, was a man in an air force uniform. Questions raced around my mind. *Who was he? Why was he here?*

I could see every detail of his clothes, every seam, every button, every insignia. It was as if a bright light was shining on him, but at the same time, he did not seem to be lit at all. Was this man a ghost? *No,* I thought, *ghosts do not exist.* He seemed solid enough to be a real man; yet no real man ever looked as insubstantial as him.

I blinked. The man had gone. One moment he was there and the next he was not. It was as though he had evaporated, disappeared into the air.

'Watch what you're doing, clumsy!' said my brother.

I glanced down. I had been pouring milk onto cereal, but had let it overflow, so preoccupied with the events of the night before. Were there really any such things as ghosts? Had I just dreamed it all?

'Did you see this?' my father asked my mother, gesticulating at the paper.

'No,' answered my mother, 'why, what does it say?'

'Well, you know the airplane that crashed around here in the war, they've found the skeleton of the pilot in a wood nearby. It says he escaped from the plane and crawled away, but died of his wounds.'

I turned to look out of the window. Could it be … ?

Eloise Liddell (14)
Prior Park College, Bath

Dear Daisy

Dear Daisy,

This letter will be placed beside you in your coffin. I am sorry for all the trouble I caused. Let's just admit it, I was jealous. You were popular, rich, pretty and had all the designer makes. I was some back-alley, drug-addicted girl, who had no father. The things I did, I never thought it would end like this. Death.

I have brought red roses for your grave. You will always be remembered at school, I won't let you lose your brilliant reputation. I hope, from Heaven, you will be able to watch me and guide me the right way and your boyfriend, no girl will ever hurt him. I am going to change. I will go and see a counsellor. I am going to turn over a new leaf and get some new clothes and a new look.

I need to confess to you now or I will never do it. The way you died, me in the corner screaming, you in the bath, your dad pushing you under and drowning you. I have always felt something for him. You remember that party you had, when you were eleven? It started then. Your mother never knew. When I missed lessons, I was with him. He fed my addiction. No one had ever cared about me. I knew one day he would hurt you, but I couldn't say.

Polly xx.

Polly Tullberg (14)
Prior Park College, Bath

Dear Mrs Robinson

16th June 1947

Dear Mrs Robinson,

It is with my sincerest apologies that I have to send this letter, but as it has to be sent, I would rather be the one to tell you. Your husband, Mr Robinson, passed away two days ago on the 14th June, from a bullet to his chest. Mr Robinson was a figure respected by us all. We all admired his skill, his courage and his care for others. It was a pleasure to spend as much time as I did with Jack, he somewhat changed me as a person. He was not only a friend, but a role model for all of his colleagues. He spoke a lot about you and I know this letter is breaking your heart and I feel so much for you.

Jack died fighting for his country, I understand all he wanted in life was to be a soldier, ever since her was a little boy. Jack has been buried, with the others, in the field of battle. He has a headstone engraved with his last words, 'I love you, Fiona'. I thought you needed to know this, Mrs Robinson. I will never forget Jack and will pray for you.

I understand that you have a child on the way, so I understand how difficult this is for you.

I wish you luck with everything. All I can do is apologise, but Mrs Robinson, my heart goes out to you.

General Smith.

Chloe Stevenson (14)
Prior Park College, Bath

I Never Saw Her Again

'Lost - one elephant, seven foot tall, average grey colourings …'

This is what we had been told to include on the posters we were making. I hadn't made a good one. I kept smudging them with my tears.

My lovely, old elephant had been stolen the night before. I knew she hadn't just run away, the whole of our circus loved her. I knew who had taken her and I was going to get her back.

I had a plan, I felt it was sure to succeed. I went to their base, an old green warehouse, with a lot of flaking paint, on the outskirts of the town. There was no one around, so I decided to go inside and have a look around for myself. I went inside, it was quiet, too quiet.

That was the last thing I remember, because the next moment I had a bag over my head and a drug injected into my arm. And now, hours later, I am still sitting here. A man came in, he said that I had been taken hostage and that unless my father agreed to take all the animals out of the circus, I would be killed.

I'm back at home now, in my old but familiar caravan. My life has changed forever. Dad had to agree to the terms that the animal rights activists made.

Now all our animals have gone. We have nothing left, except a good past, a bad present and an even worse future.

Beth Grylls (13)
Prior Park College, Bath

Stuck In Barcelona

Stuck in Barcelona, I didn't understand anything. I was stuck in a hostel with three men. My only possessions were in the bag I was hugging. I was afraid to sleep in case my bag was taken. I must have drifted off, because in the morning, that happened.

I scrambled from my bunk. The men had gone - they had taken my money and my passport. What to do? I ran to reception hoping that someone may have handed it in, no one had.

I walked out onto the streets. Without my passport, I wasn't leaving. In my pockets I found four euros - enough for a call. I looked for a phone, but it was out of order.

I felt alone; just because I'd missed my boat. I came to the beach. I sat on the sand and looked to the waves that were soothing to my mind. I tried to remain brave, but I couldn't, I realised how terrible my situation was. Alone in Barcelona, didn't speak Spanish, didn't have money or passport and no one could help.

I cried out. People looked at me. I felt like a snake behind the glass at zoos that looks so fed up, yet people still bang on the glass.

I sat on the sand and thought of something that would give me hope, but nothing came. I tried to get up and find help, I couldn't. I felt the safest I had in days and I didn't want to change that.

Emma Hetherington (13)
Prior Park College, Bath

Doomed

My hands were trembling as I held the gun. Robert was holding my other hand and telling me to run as fast as I possibly could. The moon was above me, gleaming a bright white. My dress was dirty, my petticoat was torn and I had runs in my stockings. I looks a state.

As we ran by a gated park, I threw the small weapon into a bush. I couldn't shake the image of Mr Darbington manhandling me. His eyes had been red and bloodshot and his breath had smelt of liquor.

My heart was pounding hard inside my chest, how could I have committed murder?

I could hear police whistles coming out of the darkness. Robert led me down a side street, onto a longer avenue. It felt as if the darkness was swallowing me up, the road was deserted except for a motorcar. Robert ushered me into it and told him to take us to Southampton. Robert closed his eyes and sighed heavily, at this moment I realised I loved him.

I was feeling fatigued and weak when I awoke, it was morning. We were in the docks of Southampton, I had no idea why, but I followed Robert as he dodged through the crowds. It was a cold April morning, the wind lashed at my exposed ankles.

The next thing I knew, was handing my diamond ring to a stranger in return for tickets.

Robert took my hand in his and we boarded The Titanic.

Abigail Wheatcroft (13)
Prior Park College, Bath

Cops And Robbers In Rio

Inspector Edmundo Emerson sat in his chair, pondering. Eight children had been kidnapped from the shanty towns around the city. A letter had arrived in English: *'Raise $500,000 by 12.00 tomorrow if you want to see the children again. Jardim Botanicas'*.

Edmundo's team focused on Rio's renowned drug trafficking region, Jardim Botanico. They quickly found another clue, pinned to the door of a derelict Anglican mission: *'you may seek from mall to mart, but don't forget the Devil's Heart'*.

After pondering for some minutes, Edmundo shouted out, 'Translate 'Devil's Heart' into Portuguese and you get Coraçao dos diabos, the slang name used for the volcano to the west of the city!'

By the time his police snatch team arrived at the volcano, it was already dark. Halfway up the dormant monster's side, Edmundo thought he saw a flicker of light coming from a room which for years had housed scientists assessing the volcano. Entering the dark room, the team suddenly found themselves bathed in light and looking down the barrels of a dozen guns.

'Looking for the children - or us?' the young gang leader said, contemptuously in a Nottingham accent. 'You have no interest in the children of the poor - you simply want the reward which will come from our capture. Well, we are now releasing the children and holding you for ransom - $1million, or Rio's most famous police chief dies at the hands of its newest gang - Robin's Merry Men.'

James Eatwell (14)
Prior Park College, Bath

Untitled

Ahh, finally a break, I've been saving up for a year now for this holiday. I work in a crummy building at a job I hate and the only thing getting me through this was the thought of this holiday. Boy, I don't think I would be able to last another year if something was to happ ... whoa! What was that?

The whole plane started to shake. I reached for my seatbelt and put it on fast. I heard people screaming and shouting. I turned around and saw people with scared and worried faces, encouraging each other that everything would be fine. I looked out of the window to my left, smoke was coming from the wing, now the panic really settled in. I was breathing fast and my heart was thudding uncontrollably. The speakers crackled into life, with the captain's voice telling us to put our oxygen masks and seatbelts on and not to panic. The plane was travelling extremely fast now towards the ground. The flight crew were running up and down the hallway, shouting orders and a kid was curled up and crying in the corner. We were above the water and closing in fast. I was terrified. I braced for impact, then ...

Urgh! Where am I ... ? I awoke. I was lying on what seemed to be a piece of metal floating on the ocean. I sat up and remembered the crash, but where was the plane and all the people ... ?

Giles Potts (14)
Prior Park College, Bath

An Escaped Convict

I laughed out loud as I ran for cover. I had just escaped the prison and had police close behind. My plan had actually worked! Nearby, there was a large rock. I looked back, the gates of the prison were opening. I knew I had only a few seconds. I ran as fast as my legs could take me. I dived behind the rock, as three police cars came racing out of the prison. As they drove away, I noticed a bush. There were hardly any leaves on it. I pulled and snapped a few branches to make it a temporary shelter and crawled in.

At sunrise, I crawled out of the bush and walked in the opposite direction of the prison. After about thirty minutes of walking, I was exhausted and very dehydrated. I had passed a couple of puddles of water, none of which were clean or anything near healthy. I carried on, knowing I would become extremely ill if I drank from one. Another thirty minutes, I collapsed. I couldn't go on.

Nearby, I saw another puddle. It was dirty, but I took the chance. Gasping for breath, I dragged myself towards it. I swallowed every drop of it. It tasted like the nicest drink I had ever been given. I carried on for twenty minutes, crawling for most of it. That was all I could do. I lay on the floor, lifeless. Slowly, I felt my eyes begin to shut. This was it. I was dying …

Daniel Carr (14)
Prior Park College, Bath

My Very Last Words

'I'm very sorry,' the doctor said, sympathetically.

'That's OK,' I replied, 'I know he had a great life.' I added, trying to hold the tears back.

The doctor led me to his room. I knelt by my dead father's side. 'I didn't even get to say goodbye.' I began to cry.

'I'll leave you to it. I'm sure he can still hear you,' the doctor said as he left.

'Oh, I'm so sorry, if I was here earlier, you'd still be here. It's all my fault,' I began, as I went to hold his hand. It was stone-cold. I touched it to my face. 'I have so many memories of our old days together, you looked after me so well, even when Mum died. I know it must have been so hard, looking after four children as a single dad. I always wondered why you didn't remarry.' I tried to chuckle, nothing but a smile came out.

'Do you remember when we were playing cricket in the garden and you hit the ball through Mrs Crunchman's window. She went mad, didn't she?'

I was still holding his hand. 'I hope you can hear me!'

I got up and headed for the door, I took one more glance at my father and then I left him in peace forever. My dad, my best friend and my carer had gone all in one death. I miss him and will do forever, until we meet again.

Nell Byron (13)
Prior Park College, Bath

The Man In The Moon Began To Cry

The man in the moon began to cry upon the damp sill, behind the rusty iron bars. A dim shadow was reflected upon the dark and dusty floor, as I choked in thirst and rattled the bars that blocked my only source of water. I choked in starvation, as the stale bread dried my throat and the blinding light of distant passing cars scorched my vision. I regretted everything …

Thirty years ago, I was travelling to India with my colleague, to taste the foreign flavours that Indian cooking brings. After endless battles with spicy Dhania and mangoes, I wanted to embark on an exciting adventure. My hopes were spoiled forever …

The sun had only begun to rise on my first day of travels, when I awoke to find chaos from outside my window. Below me, silk fluttered in the wind on tangled washing lines, thirty feet above, the usually busy market streets. It was eerie; the cobbled pavement remained still in the absence of scurrying shoppers.

Then I saw it, two men, faces partially covered. The killer's hand was clasped around the neck of another, whose heavy pockets spilled with gold as he crumbled against the wall, as he sank to his death, a knife in his side. By now, I had reached the scene, but before the guilty killer fled, he smothered me with the fresh blood of the victim and drenched my clothes with bitter alcohol, so that nobody, not even the police, would believe my story …

Charlotte Wilk (13)
Prior Park College, Bath

Through My Window

The rain never stopped. I thought to myself with a disappointed sigh, *I'm not going out today.* It poured down in a constant, rhythmic sound, crucifying my helpless ears. I hated the typical English weather. It always seemed to be miserable on the weekends, yet beautiful on school days. So, as I sat at my bedroom window, peering out on the agricultural apocalypse unfolding before me, I saw something I didn't expect to see.

A slightly obese, arrogant cat paraded into my field of view. It had beige and black fur, which enveloped it into a rather strange-looking ball. There was a sullen, grumpy look on his face and he sat down next to a small beech tree, sheltering itself from the dreaded rain. As it reclined there lazily, a squirrel jittered around in the branches above. The cat observed the antics of the squirrel and decided that he was suddenly rather hungry. It started slowly climbing the tree trunk in a silent, stealthy way, trying to get just a little bit closer to his next meal. Instantaneously, the squirrel noticed the feline murderer and quivered motionless for a split second. The cat knew that it was now or never, so it majestically pounced straight for the stunned squirrel.

It was the first time I had ever experienced death and it shocked me. Whilst watching this astonishing act of nature, I had completely forgotten about the miserable weather. I thought, *at least I wasn't that squirrel!*

George Mackean (13)
Prior Park College, Bath

Positive

As I looked into the child's eyes, all that I felt was pity. Her big, hazel eyes reminded me of the forest ... deep and mysterious. I slowly looked around the shabby dark room; it looked like a bomb had recently struck it, but that was an African hospital for you.

'Dr Waldorf? This is for you,' Nurse Amera kindly said. She slowly handed me the folder. It felt like cold, harsh metal, which only brought bad news. Cautiously, I lifted the lightweight folder, but this time it didn't feel light, it felt heavy with sin. Suddenly, I felt a lump in my throat, I could not swallow, the test results read: *HIV Positive.*

I shook my head in dismay. I felt like a failure. 'Come on, Steve, you can do this, you're a doctor!' I said to myself, reassuringly. On my forehead, miniature beads of sweat were collecting together and silently slid down the side of my face. I slowly looked up to see a mother cradling her sick three-year-old daughter.

'Mrs Kajkamza? As you can see, we have received the test results,' I said in a calm, yet whispering, tone of voice. The young mother looked up at me with sadness in her eyes. How could I do this without breaking her heart? But there was no turning back. I stood up straight, cleared my throat and remembered not to let my emotions get to me. After all, I am a doctor. 'Mrs Kajkamza, your daughter is HIV Positive.'

The blood drained from her face, as life was draining away from her baby. Tears were streaming down her face; she was clinging onto her child for dear life, like when a child refuses to let go of their toy. I felt that I could not let the barrier of emotion up any longer, so I carefully and discreetly let it down. One silent tear trickled down my face. I looked at the floor.

How many more times will I have to do this?

Sinéad Maya (13)
Prior Park College, Bath

Who Was In My House That Night?

One night, I was left alone, because my parents went out to see a film. I started to watch the television. I heard the front door being closed, as it was slowly creaking backwards. When the door was shut, I heard the floor creak upstairs.

Quickly, I went upstairs searching every room. I looked everywhere. I searched nearly every room, but I could not find anyone! Finally, I checked the spare room, which contained a wardrobe. Slowly and carefully, I opened the door of the wardrobe. I blinked. No one was in there. I was absolutely amazed!

I went downstairs to watch television again. Then I heard some more footsteps upstairs. I turned off the television. The footsteps got even louder. I snatched up my phone to call my boyfriend to see if I could go round. He replied yes. I put my phone down on the table, I left my phone on, so my boyfriend could hear if someone was actually nearby. I rushed out of the door and slammed the door behind me. I sprinted to my boyfriend's house.

My boyfriend was still listening down the phone. He heard footsteps coming closer. There was a long pause. He could hear heavy breathing down the phone, then a little chuckle. Then the phone went quiet.

My boyfriend called the police. When they arrived at the house, there was no break-in, nothing was stolen and there was no trace of a human footprint.

Richard Trubody (14)
Prior Park College, Bath

Flying In My Uncle's Footsteps

When I was small, my idea of a good weekend, would be spending time with my uncle Jerry. He was almost like the brother I never had. He was quite different from my father, a strict, business-like man, who I never saw without a briefcase or wearing a suit. Half the time, he was on the other side of the world, who knows where, he never told me.

It began when I was in the back of his rickety old Morris 1000, Jerry was listening to Radio 4 and hadn't talked throughout the journey. It was unlike him. He stopped the car and we hopped out. We had arrived at a small, rural airfield.

A small plane was about to take off. It turned and it propelled itself down the runway. Uncle Jerry took my hand and we hurried to the fence. He gazed at it through his spectacles. I simply beamed. I had never seen anything like it, as it left the ground, I could have exploded with excitement. It soared into the air, no strings, nothing, it was incredible. The vibration beneath my feet faded away. My uncle stood smiling at the expression on my face.

'Wanna have a go kid?'

'Ugh!' was all I could mumble.

Twelve years later, a man with tired eyes stared at the picture of his son on his mahogany desk, sadly; did he really know this boy beaming back at him? He picked up his paper. There was a short paragraph at the bottom of the page, he began to read it: *Paul Sanders, 19, has just been accepted into a top flying college. 'He's a brave boy; he always wanted to follow in his uncle's footsteps'. From a proud mother.*

Grace Denmead (14)
Prior Park College, Bath

The Horde From The Mist

Kenshi was sitting in the fields planting rice, when he heard the barbaric cries of what sounded like the Hun Horde.

He looked up to see hundreds of screaming Mongols on horses galloping towards him. He didn't know what to do. He had heard of the Huns in history lessons, but had never expected to see them in the twenty-first century.

He was stunned for a second, not knowing what to do, until he finally came to his senses, just in time to duck into a ditch and see the horses jump over him.

As he saw the last of the horses leap over him, he pulled himself up, brushed himself off and pondered over what had just happened. After several pinches to make sure he wasn't dreaming, he tried to work out what a horde of men were doing in China on horses and where had they come from?

He quickly rushed home on his small pushbike, barely breathing on the way. As he came over the last hill to his house, he saw it had been destroyed and his family trapped inside a cage, surrounded by the Hunnic warriors.

As he dropped his bike to try to find a better vantage point to see his family, he heard a horn blow and a mist swept across the land. From the mist, came an army of Chinese warriors that charged at the Huns. As the two sides were about to meet, there was a huge flash and Kenshi appeared back in the field, planting rice.

Andrew Johnson (14)
Prior Park College, Bath

The Gangster Life

'Boss, 'ow long do we 'ave to wait?'

'Till the time is right.'

That's the fifth time I had to tell Tony that. Tony is the sort who likes things quick and easy, likes to pop the target and get out. It's hard being the gang leader, I knew it was this hard, but this is like nothing I can imagine. Sure, it's easy when you're on top of things and you've got the law under your power, through bribes and terror, but when one insignificant figure then decides that he should be the main man in Chicago and tries to take me on, it's aggravating. Then he sets up a gang to contest against me! Then I've got to go and finish the pain in the neck, to set an example to the rest, to show what happens to people who try to oppose me.

I took my hat and overcoat off and lent back, since this suit was getting a bit uncomfortable. 'Not another word,' I interrupted.

A few minutes later, we saw the man we had hunted, but with a gang of men that were armed.

'Shall I call the boys?'

'Yeah, this looks like it's gonna get messy.'

So much for the quiet approach!

'Tell them to bring the Tommy guns out for a small test!'

Soon enough, they came in their cars, screeching around the bend and parked up. Everyone got out of their cars, with their Tommy guns at the ready.

'Shall we gentlemen?'

Nathan Chalmers (14)
Prior Park College, Bath

Kitchen Disasters

Theodore's passion was cooking. He would cook meals whenever he could and his meals were delicious. He was only twelve, but already a better cook than both his parents. Theodore loved to watch cooking programmes and he read cooking books. Whenever his parents hosted a party, he would cook.

His mum was going to host a party for her book club. Theodore offered to cook, wanting to try to cook a good soufflé. A soufflé is a light, spongy sweet made of stiffly beaten eggs. Theodore was looking forward to cooking, but little did he know, that it would be the last meal he would ever cook.

The first two courses went well and the feedback was positive. Theodore had made the soufflé mixture earlier, so all he had to do was put it in the gas cooker. He had been cooking for as long as he could remember and so opening the door of the cooker and putting the mixture in, was easy.

He was about to sit down, but as he did, there was a loud bang, quickly followed by a rush of heat, throwing him across the room and then he was engulfed in flames …

That was the story of Theodore. Please remember that the kitchen is a very dangerous place. Theodore had been cooking for years and all it took was a simple fault in the gas cooker to take away all that talent.

Zachary Craft (14)
Prior Park College, Bath

Life Is A Recipe

Life is a recipe thriving with flavour, but not within a book it lies. It lies within your soul and heart, where ingredients plunge and mixtures form.

As you stir, you add some butter to try to sooth the pain. How is this possible, you'll never see her again? She was the pinch of salt that missed my bowl; she was my only ounce of sweetened sugar. The sound of her powdery voice, the words she spoke, the touch of her tender hands, the vivacious smile ... I do miss her so ... but I have to keep moving forward and dive through this dough! Custard kisses and starchy hugs fill the unwanted strain. This crying mixture is poured in a pan and sizzles away. Damaged feelings float within the steam, tossing and turning like a struggling prey.

As I cut, chop, grind, sprinkly and squeeze, I mix in onion tears, I slice with bitter anger. A loving hatred builds up inside me, as I let out a silent cry. I fall to the floor in deep distress, overlooking my actions and burst into tears realising my desperate faults.

This is not just a cookery lesson, it's a time to recognise yourself and seek your hidden values. Take pride in what you do and you will be rewarded, perhaps not physically, but mentally. Once your seeds are planted deep down within your heart, you will learn to flourish.

Mother may not be with me, but she is my recipe.

Amy Wates (14)
Prior Park College, Bath

My Trip To Spain

Why are bank holidays in Spain usually busy? I was on holiday there, with my family, we had seen all there was to see - well, the beaches were our primary stopping point. We were cruising across the lands in our rented family car. Jemma and Olly were arguing, as usual. Being the oldest, I didn't get involved!

We carried on to Madrid, our final destination. It was late evening, but now the roads were quieter. We just couldn't wait to see Madrid. I was on the verge of sleeping; this was until I was blinded by a set of car lights. They were coming straight at us. Faster and nearer, until finally, *crash!* I could hear screams, then blackness swarmed over me.

A week or so later, I remember waking up in a Spanish hospital. My family were there to comfort me, even my wretched dad, usually drunken and violent, was worried. I made an attempt to sit up, however, I was constricted in my movement by tubes and other medical instruments that seemed to encircle me. I looked at my family; they were plastered in casts and bandages.

I was told then that a drink driver, who was driving on the wrong side of the road, had hit us. Unfortunately he had died in the accident. Now to me. I suppose I was the unlucky one of my family. I looked and saw the sight that I wished in my worst dreams not to see. A wheelchair.

Ed Borton (14)
Prior Park College, Bath

Secluded Without Existence

What is it to be isolated? Many say they know what it feels like. Some would say you have contacts from the outside world, others might proclaim that it's to have no friends whatsoever. It is to be remote, cut off, inaccessible, lonely. Of which, lonely is my main concern, my main upset; a description of my life - lonely.

But my type of isolation is different from others; mine is not self-inflicted, I did not want it to happen, I have not chosen to isolate myself; individuals have done that job for me. The reason why I'm left alone in the playground and why I am never invited to the birthday parties, is totally unique to any other loner in the playground.

The reason I cannot participate in sport, or ride a bike, is not because of my lack of trying, but because of my physical condition.

The reason my mother left me and my father when I was three years old, the reason is because I'm incapable of performing or functioning on my own.

I don't want sympathy, but just the chance to live my life to its fullest extent. All I wish for every night is for people to respect me; for people to like me for who I am.

The reason I am a reclusive and is not for the reason that I want to, it is because I am unable to walk, the reason is I'm in a wheelchair!

Jack Fisher (11)
Prior Park College, Bath

The Girl I Destroyed

The handgun shook gently in my hand, the power ebbing silently away. The corridor full of tainted lockers lay vacant as a decaying necropolis that had fallen into disuse. The bustling children would soon burst out of their coma-like obedience in the classroom and an overwhelming sickness enwrapped me for the slaughter.

'Are you alone Griffan, as we'd all love to join you,' Eliza said in her placid voice, riddled with devilish sarcasm and mockery.

'What do you want?' I returned, with as much dignity as the five faces pressing down on me would allow.

'We just want to know what you were up to back there,' said Will, casually stepping around me, to ensnare my entire folder. I was about to stop him, but Eliza pulled me round to face her, a grim satisfaction glimmering in her cat-like eyes.

'So, we'll see you around,' she said, the other smirking their farewells. Her hand rested on my shoulder, burning me as she stared at my pitiful existence, endorsing her innumerable actions.

I thought back to my dismal life and my heart screamed in agony. I had every right to be accepted and respected as all others in this disastrous montage of a school. The relentless hail of insults and persecution had drilled down my esteem to a zombie-like depression. This dejection had finally led me to anger and an inhuman odium of life. Things spiralled out of control the moment I could direct that anger and the consequence lay spread before me in a daunting stillness. As the colour drained from her expressionless face, very much the same happened to my soul and knowing it was the end, I turned and ran.

Benjamin Malin (15)
Prior Park College, Bath

Speaking In Front Of The Whole School

One day to go, I could not believe my teacher had picked me to speak in front of the whole school, she had only given me a day's notice. The frustration and anxiety I had in my stomach was getting too much, me, one of the shyest people had to speak, not anyone else. The teacher said I had to be prepared, but what was there to be prepared for? Apart from speaking and I guess the whole be confident thing.

All day I could not get it out of my mind. I kept thinking I would start stuttering in front of everyone, or get stage fright once I got up.

Got home, had supper, did my homework. All this kind of took my mind of it. I tried to forget about it until tomorrow and think only about this evening, but it was when I went to bed, that I had nothing else to think about that it all came back. I just sat there, listening to the butterflies flapping around in my stomach. I was trying to say to myself what was the worst that could happen? I am just reading, that's all.

Morning came, I was as nervous as anything and what was I thinking, *nothing could happen, anything could happen.* There I was, sitting by the lector, waiting for the teacher to call me up. '... she will now like to read the passage.' And I went up to the lector and looked at the school.

Holley Potts (15)
Prior Park College, Bath

The Return

'Argh!' screamed one shipmate, as the main sail of the Launcher snapped and tumbled down onto the deck, like a rage of roaring rhinoceros.

'Back to quarters!' I roared over the fierce, howling wind. Some sailors rushed to their cabins, some fell, never to get up and some tried to brave the storm, only to go overboard.

1836. I am captain of sea vessel Launcher. We are on our return to Babylon from Chile, pursued by at least 50 Chilean ships, with heavy cannon. We are running, but is our home safe?

The moonshine war. 1835-? We have been fighting in Chile, against the ferocious *Quaba*. (Chilean soldiers.)

My father is the king of Babylon, but when we received word that Babylon was being quickly overthrown by Quaba from the east, we returned. Soon, we will be home ...

Bang ... crash! Smash! The first cannon fire from our pursuers. It gashed a hole in our portside. Horror mixed with terror and adrenaline filled the hearts of men on the Launcher, as water began to seep into the cabins.

A few hours passed and finally I could see the familiar lights of the Tower House, on the edge of the Babylon pier, but I could also see smoke rising from the palace of my father. We had survived the short night, with only one attack from our attackers. We flew into the harbour, like a bullet from a gun and I jumped off the boat and swam to shore. I took out my dagger. I began to relive my training. I was ready.

I made my way toward the palace and stepped into the cool atmosphere. My father was on his throne, unconscious. I stepped toward him, but soldiers got there first. My dagger flashed, they fell. I took my father, but if he will ever wake up, I do not know.

Tom Rossi (14)
Prior Park College, Bath

The Dead And Forgotten

I looked up over the mound of moist, dank earth which had been our home for the past three months.

The gunshots had subsided to leave an eerie silence that was almost unnatural in the trenches.

Bloated bodies carpeted no-man's-land, but the sadness that I had felt in my first few weeks after losing most of my friends, had evaporated to leave feelings of hatred and anger. The soldiers on the opposite side probably felt the same hate for me, but somehow ... it was different.

I was snapped out of my trance as the gunshots started again. The night was as alive as it had been before. Rats scurried around my feet, terrified by the echoed shots.

I squinted into the blackness. I couldn't see a thing.

The rain fell in sheets so visibility was not great, in fact, it was awful.

I felt something whizz past my right ear.

Men began to scream my name. 'Shoot 'em, Joe! Joe, shoot 'em for Christ's sake!'

I supported my gun with shaking hands, but I just couldn't work out where the bullets were coming from.

My heart was no longer a steady beat, but a constant hum. Adrenaline surged through my veins. That feeling never leaves you in the desolate place that I was in.

Fear leaves you after a few weeks of being in the trenches. You begin to feel numb and a gunshot becomes an everyday noise.

There were more shots, a bright, blinding light, an excruciating pain ...

Blackness.

Beverley King (13)
Sir William Romney School, Tetbury

The Secret Garden

We were playing netball on a field in the dense woods, 'Pass me the ball, Vika!' I called. She threw the ball high into the air, it was spinning and whirling and turning towards me. The ball landed, but over the other side of a very high, crumbling stone wall.

'It's your turn to fetch the ball!' Vika joked.

I looked up at the wall. It seemed to go up and up and up. I climbed to the top. The bricks were rough on my skin. I jumped from the top, into a jungle thick with brambles and stinging nettles. It was a garden; I stumbled towards the house. I went to knock on the door, but as I did, the door slowly creaked open.

'Hello? … Um … I've lost my ball in your garden. Can I go and get it?'

There was no reply. Something made me want to explore the house, so I stepped in. The floorboards were creaky and the furniture was covered in sheets of velvet cobwebs. My mouth was dry and my palms were sweaty. As my eyes explored my surroundings, I saw a hangman's rope, hanging above the staircase. That's when I decided it was time to get out of there.

As I walked out, there was a dead body of a woman lying in front of the door. It wasn't there when I walked in. I tried to step over it to get out, but as I did, the door swung towards me and a tall man with a face as pale as snow, stared back at me. He wore a long black cloak. He stood there and stared at me. He held the door open as if to tell me to get out. I did. I thought he was going to chase me, but he just stood there and watched me, until I was completely away from the house.

Debbie-Jayne Walton (14)
The Grange School, Christchurch

Football Scout

It was a sunny afternoon in April, when my team, Twynam Rangers were playing a final match, against our rivals High Cliff Hawks. It was 1-1 at half-time. We had just started the second half when I got hacked. Matthew Nicholls took my legs outside the area. It was about 30 yards out. My other teammates told me to take the free kick. I placed the ball, took six steps back and I had a shot. It was heading straight for the top corner. It was curling in the air and it went in. We were 2-1 up.

High Cliff kicked off and they won a corner. I felt scared, because I knew they were good at corners. They took the corner and Matt was running into the box. The ball went straight to him and he dived through the air and diving - headed it in the back of the net. It was 2-2 with 15 minutes to go.

I turned round and asked the ref how long was left and he said about three minutes. I thought, *we've got to win.* One of my other teammates passed me the ball and I shot from the halfway line. The keeper was off his line and tripped over. I knew it was going in. I scored! I had won it for us. We'd won the in the cup final against High Cliff Hawks. 3-2 was the score at full-time.

At the end of the game, a strange man with a big black jacket on passed me an envelope. He said, 'Open it.' so I did. I unfolded the envelope and pulled out a letter. He was a scout. I couldn't believe it. He was a top scout from Manchester United. He said, 'Phone the number on the letter.' Then got in this black car and drove off.

When I got home and read the letter properly, it said they wanted me to have a six-week trial with them. If I was interested, I was to phone this number. I got so excited, I phoned them straight away. They said, 'Come down and meet the lads at the weekend.'

I went and everyone was nice. It was really fun and after the six weeks of hard work was over, they phoned me up and said I was in. I was really excited. It was the best time of my life, ever!

Alex Jeffery (14)
The Grange School, Christchurch

Untitled

'Argh!' screamed Natty, as she leapt out of bed, after seeing a fat, hairy spider. 'I'm gonna kill him!' He had done it again. Natty and her brother, Nick, were always playing practical jokes on each other. They would come up with the most disgusting pranks. Putting mud in each other's Coke. Pouring sand in each other's drawers. The list was endless, but a favourite of Nick's, was putting spiders in Natty's bed and that's what he had done. Natty had had enough and made a plan. Something that Nick was scared of more than anything - *ghosts!*

One night, there was a huge thunderstorm. When everyone was asleep, Natty grabbed her bed sheet and draped it over herself. She knew Nick was scared of ghosts (even though he'd never admitted it) she ran across the hall, moaning and groaning and swishing her covers. Suddenly, she felt a draft. She was getting scared herself. What was that noise?

Groans were coming from the airing cupboard. Things were getting creepy. She slowly crept up to the door, making as little noise as possible. As she burst open the door, a frightening face exploded out and let out a huge yell. *'Boo!'* Natty couldn't believe her eyes. She was petrified and ran as fast as she could, as the horrible face ran after her. Jumping into her room, gasping for breath, she slammed the door. The monster had disappeared back into the airing cupboard, but it was no monster and definitely not a ghost; it was her brother, Nick. He had played her at her own game!

Sophie Clarke (14)
The Grange School, Christchurch

A Day In The Life Of Anna

Dear John,

I got up at six this morning, fed the cat, he's getting very fat now, then I took a shower and then got dressed. I then had that porridge you love for breakfast. Then I went to see Betty in the corner shop. I still get my daily paper and have a conversation with Betty, her son's out of prison now; he was helping her in the shop this morning, filling up the shelves.

On my way home, I saw this little girl walking to school with her mother. Her hair was lovely and long and she had little red ribbons in her hair. It reminded me of when I was a little girl walking to school with my mother.

It was a lovely day today. The sun was shining all day. I sorted the garden out, all the pretty roses have come through now, it's like a little wonderland. I am coming down to visit you tomorrow; I will bring some roses from the garden with me. It doesn't get easy living without you.

Jamie came over the other day with Lauren. She is getting big now. She is the prettiest thing I have ever seen. She knows who you are. She walked in and went straight over to your picture on the wall and pointed to it and said, 'Grandad,' bless her.

Jamie and Nicky came round yesterday. They are having a baby, she is due in January and they're hoping for a little boy.

I am going to make some dinner now.

Love you and miss you loads.

Anna xx.

Kay Bowring (14)
The Grange School, Christchurch

My Short Story

In a small, rundown bungalow, George Wiener was building a machine with the intention of taking over the world. For months, George and his Wiener Patrol, had been working, with only his student next-door neighbour, Zack Hook, knowing what was going on. Zack had earlier been involved in an incident with the local tramp, Cliff, which led to a shop robbery. Zack had been assaulted by Cliff that very morning.

With a brick in one hand and a chocolate bar in the other, the enraged Cliff had broken into the Maurice Jarves' corner shop. 'Come back with my magazines!' Maurice screamed, as the gypsy waddled away from the scene.

Meanwhile, at the Wiener HQ, the machine was complete. George was taking it to the village green for testing, as an out-of-breath, angry Cliff, being chased by the police helicopter, ran straight into him.

'Get off me,' yelled George, who, by this time, had grabbed the thief.

The police cuffed him as Maurice Jarves came over to George.

'Thank you for catching the thief. You may take whatever you like from my shop, free of charge. Thank you very much!' said Maurice, who had been helping the police.

'That gives me an idea,' whispered George.

So, from that day forward, George went to work, producing various robots and selling them as 'expert security insurers'. After selling millions and making the same in money, George bought an island and retired from his money-making ways to take over the world!

Luke Lockyer (14)
The Grange School, Christchurch

A Day In The Life Of Steve

Steve is a 51-year-old car salesman, his alarm goes off at 7.00. He wakes up to see his dog lying beside him as always. He gets up, takes a shower and puts on his suit and says, 'Can't forget my lucky tie.' (A Wallace and Gromit tie.) Steve goes downstairs and starts making his breakfast, only to hear Toby coming downstairs. 'Good morning, Toby,' and gives him a pat on the head. 'Do you want your breakfast?' Toby wags his tail.

Steve leaves home at 8.00 and goes to work. He works at a local car shop, but today his boss, Dave, came up to him and just came out and said, *'You're fired!'*

Steve said, 'But? What … ?'

Steve spent the rest of the day packing up his things from his desk and said, 'The only thing that can cheer me up now, is Liverpool winning the FA Cup.'

On the way home, he made his day even worse, by crashing his car through Anne's post office window!

When Steve got home, he was greeted by Toby, who gave a faint bark. Steve went into the living room and turned on the PS2 and said to Toby, 'Maybe playing some Tomb Raider will cheer me up.' He played on it for about an hour. It cheered him up a little bit, but the highlight of the day, was Liverpool winning the FA Cup, by beating West Ham on penalties.

Sammy Speed (13)
The Grange School, Christchurch

Bad Day!

Anne woke up and got dressed. Once she was ready, she climbed on her bike and headed to work, but her bike had a puncture. 'Great!' she angrily threw the bike down and decided to walk. Her day hadn't started off well.

Once Anne arrived at the post office, where she worked, she made a cup of tea, sat down and relaxed. An hour passed and no customers had come in. Anne was very bored. A man entered the shop looking very suspicious. She kept a close eye on him. Then the man reached out and put something in his pocket.

'Excuse me, can I see your pockets please?' Anne asked.

'Certainly,' the man said.

He pulled out his empty pocket.

'Let me see the other one please.'

He put his hand in the other pocket, then suddenly started to run. Anne stuck her foot out and the man tumbled over it. She jumped on him and wrestled with him, but he was too strong and he grabbed her and pushed her to the floor.

Still shocked, she got up and saw the man running for the door. She threw a glass paperweight at his head and he fell to the floor with his head bleeding. She phoned the ambulance.

The ambulance came quickly with the police and Anne was taken for questioning. Later, she was found guilty and put in prison for attempted murder! She couldn't face what she had done.

She got a life sentence!

Chloe Etheridge (14)
The Grange School, Christchurch

Holiday In Majorca

'Wicked! We are all going on holiday in the morning,' shouted Lucy with excitement.

All the girls were sleeping round Jess' house, the night before they went to California. At 3am, all the girls were still awake. 'Come on girls, go to sleep now, you won't get up in time to get to the airport, now settle down, Jess,' mum shouted through the walls.

'OK, sorry Debz,' shouted Milz.

'Come on girls, up you get!' Dylan, Jess' little brother, jumped on all the girls to wake them up. All the girls were up, washed and dressed by ten past ten and they had to be at the airport by eleven o'clock. They rushed into the car, whacked the radio on and set off.

Kirsty, Leah, Jess, Milz, Bex, Lucy, Kay, Leonie, Gemma, Jade, Arron, Dylan, Deb and Dale were running as fast as they could to the check-in. They only had three minutes to get on the plane. They finally got there, sprinting up the aisle to reach the plane. Bex dropped her heavy suitcase, Leah rushed back to help her. They picked everything up and caught up with the others. They arrived on the plane just in time.

The air hostess said, 'Enjoy your flight to Majorca!'

'Oh no, we've got on the wrong plane!' shouted Deb.

Jess Goudie (14)
The Grange School, Christchurch

Moving House!

'I want the biggest room!' screamed Chloe. She ran upstairs and found it. Her little brother, Tom, followed. 'Get lost!'

She put her little bag in it to claim it as hers. She sat on the bed, looking out of the window. She could see people walking by smiling and laughing. Someone noticed her and stopped.

The girl on the pavement stared in horror.

Why did she seem so shocked to see me? thought Chloe.

'Chloe, come and help with the bags please darling,' shouted her mum.

She ran downstairs and went out to the delivery van taking out as many of the small bags as she could grab. She stumbled in, throwing them down and ran back outside again.

Her new house stuck out like a sore thumb! It was an 8-bedroomed house. The previous family had had the house for years and had lost three family members in it!

Chloe ran back down to the house. She opened the door slowly and climbed over all the bags, running up the curvy stairs to the end of the long, dark corridor.

'Wake up, Chloe, it's time for school now!'

'Yeah, I'm awake!' she moaned.

Chloe climbed out of bed, still half asleep and dressed in her new school uniform. After getting washed and dressed, she climbed into her car, where her mum was waiting. They arrived at their new school and walked into the gates. Everyone's eyes were upon them. They ignored them and walked into the building and found Chloe's new tutor. Her mum and little brother kissed her goodbye and went home.

Chloe walked in, everyone stared at her and she went bright red and sat down at the back of the classroom by herself. The bell rang, it was time to go to their lessons. She walked down the corridor, but couldn't find her maths class. She asked a teacher who was walking by and he took her. She walked in and all eyes glared hard at her. She smiled as her maths teacher introduced her to the class. She sat at the back, next to a girl called Jess and got out all her equipment and started listening to the teacher.

She noticed that Jess was staring at her in disbelief. She looked at her and smiled. She could still see Jess looking at her, but she ignored it.

The bell rang, time for the next lesson. She looked at her planner and saw that she had history next. Jess took her to her class.

'Where are you from?' asked Jess.

'London,' replied Chloe.

Jess stared at her, her mouth opened, but no words came out. Chloe looked at her and wondered if she was going to say anything, but she didn't. She opened her mouth again, 'I thought so.'

She showed her a newspaper and memories came flashing back. Everything went blurry and she remembered what had happened.

She was dead!

Lucy Griffiths (14)
The Grange School, Christchurch

Back To Rap

Today, me and my crew started to make a move, usually selling on corners. Little pay, long nights, but still money equals everything!

We went to get some munch. I always pay around here. I have all the money. The crew worships me. They say I'm like a god to them. They do anything and everything for me. In my spare time I sell drugs in the morning, rap at night ... whatever I feel like doing really. It's all good in my hood.

When you have a best friend, it's usually a somebody, but mine is a gat 99 ... always by my side. See, we have to protect ourselves from the Columbians, our worst enemies, who live right next door to us ... well, practically.

My occupation wasn't to rap or sell drugs. I was brought up into a rough way of living. I didn't know my dad. I lived with my mum, but most of the time I was at Grandma's. I knew my mum sold drugs ... I mean, she always had money. As long as she kept selling the drugs, I got my sneakers for school. Sneakers are everything!

My father could be anyone ... who knows? My mum was meant to come home that night ... but didn't. The neighbour said their was screaming next door. Then the smoke came.

Those four years, sleeping in the basement at Grandma's were OK I suppose. My grandad found my gun. I was stitched, wasn't thinking that day when I went back to school, so I decided to leave my grandma's house and find one of my own. Back to rapping.

Grant Ritchie-Haydn (14)
The Grange School, Christchurch

Mrs Lollipop

It's very early in the morning and Mrs Lollipop wakes up and draws open the curtains to let in the morning sun. She goes to wake up her daughter, to tell her to get ready for school. She then goes downstairs and makes her husband his morning coffee. He likes his morning coffee, he cannot go to work without it and he likes it strong with only a spoonful of milk. He then goes off to work in his red sports car. Her daughter then comes downstairs and has her breakfast, tidies up her hair, kisses her mum goodbye and skips off to school.

Mrs Lollipop then puts her feet up and watches EastEnders. She likes EastEnders and can't wait until her family gets home so she can make the dinner, that's her favourite part of the day. Tonight is roast pork night. She has to make sure it's in the oven by 3.00.

She decides to do some cleaning and as she is cleaning she notices one of her ornaments is missing and in the space where it was, there is a note saying, *Follow.* As she follows the house gets darker and darker. She has never seen this part of the house before. She sees another clue saying, *Come In,* so she opens the door and notices some blood on the floor, then she screams and that's the end of Mrs Lollipop.

Rebecca Seymour (15)
The Grange School, Christchurch

FA Cup Final

All my mates got tickets for the West Ham - Liverpool game, we couldn't wait to go. Six more days to go.

We arrived at the stadium, then we walked up the steps and peered over the chairs and the people looked around.

At half-time the atmosphere had changed as Liverpool were losing 1-0. It changed the mood of people shouting and pushing. It soon started to get out of the police's hands, but then the teams came out and all the fans were shouting.

Halfway through the second half, it all started again, because West Ham scored a fantastic goal, which put them 2-0 up. Liverpool got one back from an own goal and the place hit the roof, all the Liverpool fans were laughing at us, then ten minutes from time, they scored again, 2-2.

How did we let it go? All of a sudden, *bang!* The ball hit the back of the net. 3-2 West Ham scored. The West Ham fans roared, while the Liverpool fans went crazy and this time they had to keep the lead.

The final score was 3-2 and then it was the end of the match. West Ham had won the FA Cup for the first time in years and the fans cheered when they lifted the cup. I felt excited, I had waited for this day for ages and now it is West Ham's time to shine.

Adam Burtenshaw (14)
The Grange School, Christchurch

My Short Story

I woke up after a long nap. It was 7.30 and my best friend, Darling, normally cooked me lunch, but she wasn't there. I kept hearing screaming and shouting coming from the bedroom across the hall. This normally happened about this time; he gets in, eats, has a beer and starts shouting at her. So, as usual, I waited and waited. It got to 8.00. I started to become impatient, so I went to get my own food.

I got out of bed and skipped down the hallway and I looked up and on the side there was my dinner. So, I climbed up on the side (using all my strength) and started to eat what I think was meat. The food they made for a family member was terrible; it looked like cardboard smothered in brown glue, but I still ate my fill and got down.

I decided to sit in my chair and enjoy the peace and quiet. Wait a minute, it's quiet! A sudden rush went up my body and all my hair stood on end, daringly I growled. I ran down the hallway into their room, when suddenly he grabbed me and threw me across the room. I heard Darling scream, 'No!' but the room started to spin and I was out cold.

I woke up later. I couldn't believe he done this. I gave him all my love. I mean, how could someone hit a cat?

Rosy Conner (15)
The Grange School, Christchurch

Aang's Great Tale Of Time

There was a great battle, thousands of years ago, between the fire, earth, air and water nations. A young boy named Aang was hiding in his house, keeping out of the battle. Suddenly, he heard the front door swing open. He hid under his bed. He heard someone call out his name, but he didn't reply. He heard them coming towards his bedroom. The door swung open. It was Yatugo, his father.

Yatugo took Aang down into the basement and had a long talk with him. He thought it was the right time to tell Aang that he was the chosen one. Aang was confused. He flew through the roof and made a hole in it. He was flying around and was caught in a storm. He couldn't handle it, so he flew back. He tried so hard to escape, but he couldn't. Suddenly, he was struck by lightning and went falling into the sea. He concealed himself inside a bubble of ice.

Hundreds of years passed, then the bubble was seen by Zoran and Hygo when they were fishing. They went over to see what it was; Hygo wasn't over keen on it. Zoran stole Hygo's weapon and whacked it. It started to glow from inside, then suddenly, they were sent flying into the water and the bubble cracked open. They climbed out of the water and Aang was just sitting there …

Ashley Long (13)
The Grange School, Christchurch

Izuru's Tale

Welcome reader, if you wish to hear my story, then here it is, the story of Izuru, the warrior.

This story starts with a great battle, the greatest gathering of armies ever. All to fight and kill me. Each of the armies is controlled by an evil lord; of earth, wind, fire and water. To them I was a threat, but their power could not rival mine.

I slaughtered all that came before me until none but the lords themselves were left. Then it happened. They all blasted a great beam at me, which froze me as a statue. All knowledge escaped me. I could not think, I could not breathe. For them, they were victorious and I was cast into an everlasting shadow of doom and to be released, someone must chant the incantation, 'Durnan bygan degoran benan'. But in English this means, 'I wish to be free'. Eventually, a candle of hope in the darkness came and that candle was Max.

5,000 years later, I became the emblem for a school called The Grange. I was put up on the school roof to be seen for miles. Max came and hid on the roof from the bullies. He ran over to the statue crying, saying, 'I hate my life!' Then he said it, 'I wish to be free!' in a brilliant flash of light, my stone casing was destroyed and I was free …

Scott Butcher (13)
The Grange School, Christchurch

The Forbidden Barn

The moon was whole and the breeze in the air rattled the old barn gates. The used straw was rotting in the days of freshly spread dew and the two dealers were secretly perched on the fresh barrels on hay.

'Right, where's my stuff? I got your money, now give me my stuff,' one of the dealers demanded in a dominant voice.

'I'm sorry, but my actions in getting your request has been delayed due to insufficient contacts,' the other one replied, in a mysteriously intelligent voice.

'What the hell are you on about?' the other one replied, viciously.

As he began to raise his fists, his partner interrupted and said, 'I'm ever so sorry, but I haven't managed to get your drugs.'

He struggled to sustain his calm voice, under the pressure of his intimidated partner.

The large man lifted a gun out of his back pocket and gradually pulled the trigger back and then rested his finger on the edge of the gun. He waited. His scared victim fell to the ground, clutching his wound in pain. He lay on the cold wooden floor and gazed into the other person's eyes. Blood poured from his mouth.

'Why?' his eyes closed as he held onto his last and final breath of air.

Jason Ambrose (13)
The Grange School, Christchurch

The Journey

The sand was as hot as fire. Our shoes were filled with sweat and were disintegrating off our feet. I fell onto my knees and reached for my gourd to find a last drop. I looked ahead of me to see Kae still walking in front of me. Beyond my blurry vision, I saw smoke, far away. I opened my mouth, but all I could do was gasp for air. I managed to shout, 'Smoke!' Kae fell flat on his face. I blacked out.

I was woken by the sound of drums echoing through the tunnels of a large, damp cave. I moved my arm to find it was sealed to the wall in rusty chains, they seemed fragile, but I had run out of energy. I heard echoing shouting in foreign languages and lifted my head to see orange light flickering in the tunnels ... Kae stumbled in wounded, in his left arm he wielded a large bone. Hastily, he lifted his arm and broke the chains, I fell onto my hands and knees and smacked my elbow on a sharp rock.

'Get up!' Kae screamed.

The orange lights grew closer, the shouting louder. I grabbed the large rock, stood to my feet and waited. Kae mumbled to himself, 'I wish we'd never looked for this place!'

Suddenly, a number of odd tribe-looking men stumbled in. I threw the rock at one of them, killing him instantly. I turned around to see my companion dead. Picking up his bone, I swung it overhead into one's face, he caught it and smiled, jabbing a spear in my chest. Once again, my vision faded.

Jake Kneale (15)
The Grange School, Christchurch

Scarecrow

Pale clouds drifted in the sky, covering the cold full moon. A haunted house in the country, surrounded by creepy-looking trees. The rumours were that if you entered, you wouldn't come back out. In the crop field, a dark figure stood in the shadows. A scarecrow, but not an ordinary scarecrow. Once in a while, it sprung to life.

Five years ago there had been two travellers who took a wrong turn and found themselves at the farm. They had never heard of the rumours. Both of them saw the scarecrow and walked past it. The girl looked back - it was gone! Frightened, they both ran off. The girl ran ahead and looked back, he was gone! Hearing footsteps closing in, she turned, there it was! She screamed, the last anyone heard of her.

Sam and Dean were brothers, ghostbusters if you like, they arrived in town. Sam noticed the pale, cold full moon and spotted a house in the mist. They headed towards it. Dean had left his equipment in the car, a mistake. After hearing strange noises around, Dean turned back, the shadow figure of the scarecrow had gone. He tried to warn Sam, but Sam was gone too. Dean ran back to the car, picked up his gun and tried to catch up with Sam.

As Dean ran, Sam was trapped by the scarecrow blocking his way. The scarecrow held a steel hook and was about to kill Sam there and then. Hearing Sam scream Dean's name, Dean aimed his gun at the scarecrow and fired.

Screams can still be heard from the farm to this day.

Laura Dauncey (14)
The Grange School, Christchurch

The Beast

One stormy and dark evening, Roger was going home from work. As usual he walked, this time in the rain, holding an umbrella over his head. Opening the door, he noticed that the lights were flickering and everything had been overturned in the rooms. He went upstairs and looked around, it was the same.

Just before he could turn around, something shot past him. He slowly tiptoed towards the other room, with the floorboards creaking. He slowly opened the door and there it was, *the beast!*

It had huge tufts of spiky hair, big enough to reach the ceiling, with three multicoloured eyes and massive sharp teeth. Roger stared for a moment, then slammed the door shut, locked it and ran.

Immediately he heard a bang from upstairs, but he didn't worry about it, he believed the beast was safely locked up. Going into the kitchen to put the kettle on, he heard a repulsive growl behind him. He slowly swivelled round and there it was again. Roger backed away, till his back connected with the back door. He ran out and called the police and they arrested the beast.

After that, his home was fine and so was he.

Cameron Collins (12)
The Grange School, Christchurch

It

It came, it went. It comes and goes. What is it; we all want to know what it is. It is a mere projection of what our mind creates and who am I to say what mind creates is the truth. But what is truth? Truth is it and it is truth. When you find out what it is, is the day when you become it. But why do we ask ourselves, what is it? It is everything and nothing, it is there when you are, it is there when you're not. But, although you created it, it also created you. But why is it here? It is here for a purpose, a purpose that it can fulfil. But when it does, is when it is the purpose. It will take you; consume you, until it is consumed by you. You can't destroy it, unless you destroy yourself. But it can't exist if there is nothing to create it and you're not there for it to create. You just have to remember one thing ...

It will always be there.

Sam Adams (12)
The Grange School, Christchurch

The Tale Of Tor And Steven: Guitar Gods!

'Jam for your life!' Steven cried.

Tor grabbed his guitar and licked a face-melting solo. Herman, the evil monkey, got blasted into the vortex of the Fragile Alliance. 'I'll get you, Tor and Steven!' Herman screamed.

'That's the last time that monkey will try to steal the jam, Tor,' said Steven, triumphantly.

'Yes, Steven,' chirped Tor, 'let's go out on our pink mopeds.'

Just then, the vortex of the Fragile Alliance opened. Out jumped a man with a fat head. 'Ha, ha!' he laughed. 'I am Sam, the evil ruler of the Fragile Alliance!'

'Holy CJ and Tab!' Tor yelled.

'I'm here to steal all that is rock and maybe a little roll!' Sam chuckled.

Suddenly, a billion coloured dots flew into the room.

'What are these?' said Sam, blinded by the colours.

'They're Action Tab dots!' said Steven, with a laptop around his neck.

'Nooooooo!' Sam wailed, blown away by the dots.

The whole room blew up. Tor and Steven flew up in the air and landed on a concrete slab, left there by Black Zeppelin.

Tor and Steven woke up on what seemed like a fluffy bed. A man wearing ripped spandex and his arm falling off, came over to them. 'Hi, I'm LP Freak. Welcome to Heaven! Have you seen my wife? I've lost her.'

Liam Talbot (13)
The Grange School, Christchurch

The Leaf That Dies

People can see me, but they never hear my voice. I hear all, but I never speak. Not a word. Not a whisper.

I sit here, hanging limply from a branch, watching all the insects crawling and climbing, up the brown, broken bark of my dry summer tree. People walk past me, children play with my old friends, as they have fallen to the ground. I do not miss them as I have many others, for a tree always grows new leaves for the coming months. I wonder when I might fall. When my pigment fades and I will turn brown like the tree I live on.

I stay here alone, but not for long as a little ladybird comes looking for aphids. Unluckily for him my body is clean as I avoid pests but I do not know how. They never come to me, which is why I still hang waiting for the day I will be chewed by bugs and will die.

The ladybird flies away, as he does, so I feel weak. It has started. I'm drained of energy. My veins are weak and as I look at my browning skin, I begin to let go. Not that I want to, but my time has come to join my fellow friends and become a dead being. I fade darker; I am gone, never to see the happy children, but to be played with like an old broken toy at the back of a cupboard. So I say goodbye.

Caroline Martin (12)
The Grange School, Christchurch

Chill Wind

A chill wind blew through the trees. Leaves covered the floor and were dyed red. Bugs ran over a body of a 13-year-old girl called Emma. Caterpillars crawled around the mouth. Her arms were outstretched with cuts all down them, with blood dripping slowly and mixing with the earth.

Suddenly, out of the eerie silence, came shrill screams, as Vicky a 14-year-old girl and Chloe, her friend, came across the pale, zombie-like body. Meanwhile, a rustling came from some nearby bushes. Two gunshots masked the screaming.

One week later, three bodies were found in dustbin bags floating by Avon beach. The arms, legs and heads had been amputated. A funeral was held for all three girls and thunder and lightning filled the sky and the windows cried with rainwater.

2007 came and a man called Jake was arrested with a life sentence in jail. After that life was never the same, but for Jake, there was no life. Later on that day, his body was found hanging from a hook by a chain and cuts up his arm. In his mouth was a letter, explaining how the guilt had got to him for murdering innocent young girls.

Helen Smith (12)
The Grange School, Christchurch

The Mexican Pension Pincher

The room slowly came into focus. It had been a rough night for Rafael. He looked up to see a strange Chinese man staring at him. The Chinese man raised his broom, ready to attack him. 'Wait!' cried Rafael. 'I can get you money!'

The Chinese man lowered his broom and asked, 'How?'

'We can go to the retirement home back in my hometown. Where are we?'

'We are in a sacred Chinese temple, in Hong Kong. How did you get here?'

'I can't remember. What's your name?'

'Dau Ning Wang. I'm a cleaner at the sacred temple.'

'Great, let's go to the airport.'

'OK Rafael, let's go get lots of money!'

A long plane journey later, the pair arrive in Mexico.

'Wow, how did I manage to get all that way in one drunken night?' questioned Rafael.

'What date did you get drunk?' Dau Ning Wang asked.

'First of April, my friend, April Fool's Day.'

'Today is the 5th of April. How have you been drunk for so long?'

'I don't know my Chinese friend, but it sure was fun. Enough chatting, let's go and get rich!'

'OK!'

Outside the retirement home for Mexican Super Nannies

'Inside that house, the old women are loaded!' whispered Rafael.

'But there are young girls with the grannies,' Dau Ning Wang stated.

'OK, we'll wait till they go.'

Inside the home …

'Alright mother, I'm going. I'll visit you again tomorrow.' Said Elizabeth.

'Yes dear,' replied her mother.

Outside again …

'Right, she's gone, let's do this quickly,' Rafael said.

'So how do with split the takings?' Dau Ning Wang asked.

'We don't!'

Bang!

Jonathan Bakes (15)
The Grange School, Christchurch

Ghost Story

'They had been there for hours, so it seemed and no one dared to get out and switch the light on, even though that was the only thing that would make 'it' go away. The only thing that would dispel the evil that lurked in their bedroom'.

'Why don't you turn the light on, Bethany? You're the closest!'

'I'm too scared,' said Bethany.

Sophie said, 'You're scared, I'm not ever, is Georgia, are you Georgia?'

'No not really,' said Georgia.

Then out of the blue Bethany said, 'Did you hear that?'

'No,' said Georgia and Sophie.

Then they all heard a scary noise and screamed.

'What was that?' said Georgia.

'We don't know,' said Sophie and Bethany.

Every now and then the noise would come back.

'I'm never sleeping round yours again Georgia, well, until you get this sorted,' said Bethany.

'Yeah, Georgia, I agree with that!' said Sophie.

After Sophie had said that, they all ran out of the room and ran into Georgia's brother, Sam and his mates, Luke and Garry. They came into Georgia's room and they all screamed and Georgia's mum ran up to see what had happened.

Georgia said, 'They have been scaring us.'

'How?' Mum said.

'They have been making scary noises,' said Bethany.

'Yeah and they have been calling our names,' said Sophie.

'Why did you do that, Sam?'

'I don't know, we were bored.'

'Yeah, well, we were scared,' said Georgia.

'Leave your sister and her mates alone and you leave your brother and his mates alone.'

'OK!'

'Yes, Mum!' Georgia and Sam said.

Georgia-May Davis (12)
The Grange School, Christchurch

A Day In The Life Of A Rally Car

I got to the garage where the Subaru was and I got into the transformation box and I was transformed into the car. My eyes were the headlights, my top grille was my nose, the bottom grille was my mouth, my ears were the wing mirrors and my hair was the decals. All of a sudden, I felt a little rumble and I was off, being driven by Petter Solberg. I didn't feel too many bumps and lumps, but it was a little bit uncomfortable. I didn't like it when I was driven up the hill and my tyres were just dropped to the ground and the suspension bounced wildly. The rest of the time was being driven into the pits, but one of the pit crew was very, very quick so that I didn't feel a thing. I didn't like my tyres being ripped off, I could go anywhere and I panicked and my engine failed. The thing is, I have to be driven very fast.

Now for the rest of the day; I was racing another twenty-nine Subarus around the track. Jeremy Clarkson was driving an STI like me, but I was a lot faster, because I was being boosted before each race. I liked being driven round and round in circles, though my tyres were getting very sore and I was getting very tyred (get the joke?)

Oh dear, I was getting frustrated and angry with the surface of the road. It was covered in oil to see how well the cars handled the different conditions. So I had to go to the garagital (like a hospital, but for cars). I had a really sore grille because flies and grit had flown in it; it tasted absolutely disgusting.

It was absolutely fabulous and if you ever have the chance to do this, then I suggest you take that opportunity.

Sam Sprinks (12)
The Grange School, Christchurch

The Mystical Island

Ben was a boy. He lived in the town of Christchurch between Bournemouth and Southampton and he loved sailing on his homemade raft with his best mate called Simon. The raft had a sail made of a bedsheet and a mast made of plywood. One day he was sailing around the harbour, when a strong current grabbed his raft. Everything instantly went foggy and Simon yelled. Ben noticed the sail had gone limp and it appeared that they were not moving at all. Suddenly, a jagged chunk of coral smashed through the bottom of the raft and Simon screamed as it sliced his shin.

'Why is there coral in the middle of Christchurch harbour?' wondered Ben, but as suddenly as it had started, it stopped. Simon was still screaming.

'It's stopped, it's stopped,' Ben said softly to himself. He looked around and gasped. He, Simon and his raft were stuck on a coral reef surrounding a tropical island.

Ben blinked and rubbed his eyes. He thought he could see figures gathering on the beach. Some were waving, some yelling and some wielding primitive spears and knives. Ben dragged Simon off the raft and started to swim towards the island. Suddenly, a canoe sped past him; strong hands grabbed him and Simon and hoisted them out of the clear sea. Ben suddenly felt very drowsy and fainted.

When Ben awoke, he sat up and spewed up loads of seawater, suddenly he heard a deep, husky voice saying, 'He wake up, we feed god.'

Ben quickly got to his feet, he had visions of films where cannibals sacrificed stranded sailors to a volcano or something.

'Do as god wishes,' said that deep voice.

There were loads of people gathered there now, all bowing down to him.

'Me? God?' stammered Ben. 'OK, if you will do what I want. Send me home!'

Suddenly there was a flash of light and Ben was soaking wet. He opened his eyes. He and Simon were floating in the middle of Christchurch harbour. Simon's leg was not spewing blood anymore and there seemed to be no proof of what had happened, except when he saw his raft. There was a jagged chunk of coral wedged through the middle of the raft. It would never sail again.

James Shannon (11)
The Grange School, Christchurch

The Shoebox

The shoebox was glowing blue up in the attic.

I walked past to find a shoebox jumping around. I was so scared, I fell off the ladder onto the floor.

The very next day I woke up in hospital to see the exact same shoebox right there, next to me, on the bedside table. I nearly leapt out of my skin. 'Argh! What the hell is that doing here, Mum?'

'Um, I'm not sure honey.'

Everyone was gone and it glowed again …

Daniel Mark Walker (12)
The Grange School, Christchurch

Horror House

It was a cold, dark winter. In the middle of a deserted forest was a small haunted house. Me and three mates were going camping for two days. We were walking into the forest when we came across a little house with cardboard over the windows. It was covered in ivy weaving up the building. It looked really creepy. The door was open. We went inside.

Inside there were cobwebs hanging off the ceiling. Spiders creeping over the floor. There was a small kitchen inside with knives hanging on hooks, an empty jar of jam with mould and little bugs crawling over it. We all walked upstairs and there was one bedroom.

Inside were two big beds. The covers and sheets were rotten. Holes in the floor and there was a scruffy teddy bear sitting on the pillow. There was a baby's mobile hanging on top of the bed.

We got our sleeping bags out and started getting ready for bed. We all thought about who must have lived here. Someone must have died.

We were all going to bed and I was the only one that couldn't sleep. I felt a cold breeze pass through me along with smoke. I shook with fear. It must have been a ghost!

All of a sudden, my feet felt like they were being tugged. They started to get pulled in the air. I tried to stop it but something was pulling and it wouldn't stop. An old lady walked through the door and I screamed, then everyone wake up and the smoke disappeared. The old lady walked out.

What was going on?

Tiffany Grant (13)
The Grange School, Christchurch

The Woods

One night, walking in the dark, gloomy woods alone, I heard an owl screeching in the biggest tree as if it was trying to get my attention.

My heart raced to a fast beat and I began to panic. I felt the worst was going to happen. I carried on thinking to myself, *it's alright, I'm gonna be fine!* Before I knew it, a hand grabbed my mouth and dragged me to the ground. I looked up to the top of the tree and saw the owl, I knew something was up.

The stranger kept his hand tightly over my mouth. He turned me round and stared into my eyes, deadly. I could feel the pumping in my head as if I was going to die! I struggled as hard as I could, but he dragged me through the undergrowth to a dark place in the middle of the woods. He handcuffed me to a piece of wood that was standing and ran out. I didn't know whether I was going to live or die …

Heather Burton (13)
The Grange School, Christchurch

Street

Heavy fog hugged the street whilst the lights flickered on, casting a dull glow over the empty street.

Chris was walking his dog as his punishment for being a bad boy at school and getting suspended. Chris could hear footsteps behind him. He didn't think anything of it, so he carried on walking. Chris stopped to light his fag. He could feel someone breathing behind him on his ear. As Chris turned around, the man turned around and ... *whoosh!* The man sliced Chris in the face several times.

Chris was laying dead in the streets for hours. At 6am a jogger saw Chris and phoned an ambulance. It was too late. Some people say Chris still walks the street as a spirit of the night. Waiting for his teacher to return.

Adam White (14)
The Grange School, Christchurch

Untitled

The night was like a dark velvet. On the very dark, narrow country lane, there lived a house, the only house which was miles away from any other. This house was a farmhouse. It had a stable and was built in the 1600s. It was for sale for a very cheap price. It was for sale for six months. People would come and go, but strangely, no one would want to buy the house. Eventually a couple who had a young daughter and two sons needed a big house because they wanted to start a new life. They went to the estate agents to put an offer in and they straight away accepted it and the keys were handed over. They were so pleased, that they moved in but before they settled in, they asked why the six-bedroom mansion was for sale at such a cheap price, was there a catch?

The estate agent lady stuttered and eventually told them the truth; the family who used to live there became crazy and killed each other. They were shocked but didn't think there would be any harm.

It was a long night and the couple, Jane and Pete never told their children about what had happened at this house. The kids were Jane's children and Pete was just a boyfriend. James, Jane's oldest son had never like Pete. They all eventually got to bed and the couple saw that there were certain items left in the house, for example, the clock, it was broken and was stuck on 3 o'clock. Pete fixed it and then went to sleep. The clock was working fine.

It was 2.55, the windows were closed, but the curtains were moving. The window in the bedroom had fingerprints on like someone was breathing heavily on the other side of the window. It turned 3 o'clock and the window blew open and Pete woke up. He was sweating but in less than two minutes he began to get cold. He closed the window and stared at the clock. It was 3 o'clock.

He went down the stairs to get a glass of water. As he walked across and down the stairs, they creaked. He turned the light on in the kitchen. He opened the fridge and then the light started flickering. He stood on the chair to fix it, but what he didn't realise was that there was a dead girl behind him. She was pale with long blonde hair. She had cuts on her face and her mouth was split wider. He heard a girl singing so he turned round and saw nothing. He began to try and fix the light and he heard it louder. He turned round, again nothing was there. He heard it louder behind the back of his chair. It suddenly stopped. His heart pumped slower, sweat dropped down his face and the room was quiet. All he heard was the light flickering. Pete slowly turned round, thinking nothing of the noise and the girl stood in front of him. He screamed and smashed the light bulb. He fell in the water on the floor. His heart was beating faster than a jackhammer. He tried to find his lighter. The dead girl was still there even though he couldn't see her. She screamed with a screeching voice. He moved quickly and slipped because of the water on the floor. He knocked his head on the table and he blacked out. The girl started giggling and moved up the stairs …

William Parkinson (13)
The Grange School, Christchurch

The Ice Cube

It was a cold and frosty evening and The Marina along with its crew and Becky (who didn't know what she was doing there) were sailing across the North Atlantic ocean, towards America. The captain, Krissy, was enjoying a mug of hot cocoa topped with cream and marshmallows in her study.

All of a sudden, there was a massive crash and the whole boat shook vigorously. Krissy's cocoa was poured all over her lap. 'Damn it!' she exclaimed, mopping herself up. She put her mug down on the table, stood up out of her armchair and marched out onto the deck.

'What on earth was that?' she demanded.

'Well, there was like this really big ice cube thing and I think we might have hit it!' Becky replied, twisting her strawberry bubblegum around her finger.

'So we've hit an iceberg?' Krissy asked, starting to lose her temper.

'Like dah, that's what I said,' Becky exclaimed. She thought for a few seconds then excitedly burst out, 'So are we going to die then?'

Getting extremely annoyed, Krissy shouted, 'You always have to look on the bright side don't you!'

Catherine Palmer (14)
The Grange School, Christchurch

Photo Booth

January 5th 2003, I was on my way to having the best holiday or so I thought. Sitting on the platform with my mum and dad, watching the times on the board on the other side, when I spotted a photo booth. I begged my mum to let me have one and eventually she gave in. I sat down and smiled for four photos, hearing my train being called, I grabbed my pictures and ran.

Once on the train, I flicked through my pictures to have a good look and was amazed to find that the last one didn't look like me at all, but was a picture of a girl with a yellow face. I was scared and quickly put them away.

An hour later the train began to shake furiously, passengers screamed and cried out all around me. I couldn't see my parents anywhere; suddenly, suitcases fell on top of me. That's all I remember.

I woke up in a hospital bed with my auntie and uncle beside my bed; they explained to me that my parents had been killed in the train crash. They had been burned as a result of a fire.

A nurse came round with dinner trays, I couldn't eat, glimpsing my reflection in horror. There she was, the girl with the yellow face.

Melanie Groves (15)
The Grange School, Christchurch

The Call

Once upon a time there was a fifteen-year-old girl called Frank who was a babysitter and one time she was looking after five innocent little children whose parents were out on the town. They were careless parents and only cared about themselves. Anyway, Frank was looking after these kids when the phone rang. *Beep, beep*, Frank happily walked towards the phone and answered it, only to hear a mysterious voice say, 'I'm going to kill you, then hang you on the church tower,' panted the dark, deep-sounding voice.

Beep, he'd hung up.

Frank quickly dialled 999 and told the police about the phone call. They traced the call and rang. Frank waited nervously. She picked up only to hear a rushed voice say, 'Quick, get out of the house. The call is coming from upstairs, quick, get out!'

The thing is though, the house was a bungalow …

Sam Mills (12)
The Grange School, Christchurch

My Life In The Countryside!

It was deserted, nothing around, no one around. It was like being locked in a room by yourself and never being able to unlock the door. It was, well, the countryside, what do you expect?

I missed Poole, it was so together, everyone always spoke to each other and every Saturday I would go shopping and there would be people everywhere, it was so noisy, but I was used to it, but it's so different in the countryside. I used to wake to the smell of fuel, the sound of children screaming and cars rushing by, but now it's the sound of the birds singing, the smell of cows and countryside.

I like playing the country girl, but I now I grew up with a bear belching dad and a stroppy sister.

My only saviour was a small town a couple of miles down the long, windy lanes and a small village hall which was used for a small school every day (it was a good school though).

All I heard each day was *clip clop, clip clip* of horses' hooves and the little birds singing happily on the wavy branches of the family apple tree that was already there when we came.

I love the countryside and this is where I will bring up my children and they will bring up theirs and so on, because the countryside is a beautiful place.

Jessica Barrett (12)
The Grange School, Christchurch

The Danger Of The House

There's a dark, overgrown forest in the middle of nowhere and in the woods there's a big haunted house. Sarah, a young girl, who lives nearby, thought she would take a stroll in the woods with her dog, Pippin. What she didn't know was that there's a haunted house.

She stopped and let Pippin off the lead and threw a ball for her to fetch. Ten minutes later, Sarah started to get concerned because her dog hadn't returned. She called Pippin but there wasn't any sign of her. So she walked deeper into the woods and continually called, 'Pippin?'

She then soon came across the big haunted house and the door was wide open. Sarah wasn't sure if Pippin was in there. Sarah then slowly and quietly walked up to the house and peeped her head round the door. Pippin was there.

Sarah ran in the house and grabbed her and said, 'Never run away like that, you got me worried.'

It was then, when they were about to leave, that the door slammed shut. Sarah was frightened, but thought it may have been the wind, but she walked up to the door and pulled hard, but the door wasn't opening. She didn't know what was going to happen. Will they ever get out ... ?

Megan Byrne (14)
The Grange School, Christchurch

Football

It was a sunny Sunday afternoon when my team Highcliffe Hawks were winning 4-0 and I had scored all four. It was a magical day for me, everything was going right. The full-time whistle went and we had beaten our rivals, Burton. As I was about to go home and relax, I was approached by a rather tall man. I was quite nervous as he was walking towards me and shouting, 'Wait!'

When he got close to me, he started to clap and I didn't know what to think of it. He pulled out his wallet and got out his card. It said, 'Southampton Scout'. I couldn't believe my eyes. He wanted me to go on a six-week trial period. I was speechless, I just didn't know what to say, except thank you very much and my mum was so happy for me, she thinks I deserve it.

As soon as I got home, I rang everyone. My dad, my nan and grandad and all my mates. Everyone was so pleased for me. it was great.

Six weeks later the trials were great. I got in and all my teammates were very nice to me and understanding during my trial period. I am now playing for the first team and scoring plenty of goals and in a year's time, I will be playing for Southampton in the Championship and then you never know what will happen after that.

I think that football is about luck as well as being talented because you have to be lucky to be seen and scouted and after that, your talent will guide you.

Matt Nicholls (13)
The Grange School, Christchurch

The Hooded Figures

Dave was walking down the road when a car pulled up, a hooded figure dived out and started firing at the horrified man who just managed to jump into an alleyway and dodge the bullets, he then ran for his life towards an abandoned warehouse. The hooded men in the car followed by foot but lost sight of him. Eventually they thought the only place he could have gone was the warehouse, so they wandered in with caution.

As they wandered in a hooded figure whispered, 'You take the left side, I'll take the right.'

Dave heard the echo of this whisper and he decided he would try and fight his way out.

Dave decided that he would attack the man on the left because he knew he had a gun and he was the smallest of them both. He found a lead pipe and he hid in the shadows and waited for the hooded figure to reach him. Once the man came, Dave swung the lead pipe straight at his head and knocked him clean out. So he took the gun and shot the other man, who had just come round the corner.

Jordan Purchase (13)
The Grange School, Christchurch

The End

A cold silence crept slowly around the forest. The figure's feet crunched the snow beneath them, he looked around cautiously. I continued walking my path knowing we would meet at some point, the air was crisp and a feeling of loneliness surrounded me. As I continued walking leaves brushed my face in the wind and the trees hung oppressively above me. As we moved closer, I grew more nervous but I wasn't going to show it, I wasn't afraid. The figure stopped dead in front of me, it was wearing a long hooded robe, its face covered in darkness. A sense of despair surrounded him. I stood waiting; he turned his head to the side and removed a hand from his pocket. It was pale and grasping a dagger. Turning to face me, he had the instinct to kill. What should I do?

Miles McAllister (13)
The Grange School, Christchurch

The Night Monster

It was a dark and stormy night in the graveyard as booms of thunder cracked the sky with their loudness. Flashes of flash lightning lit up the entire graveyard so that you saw all the gravestones clearly. As the sky lit up you saw a figure creeping into the house in the middle of the graveyard.

It looked like it was wearing a black hooded coat and long baggy trousers which looked like jeans. The figure entered the house and crept up the stairs without making a single noise not even a stair creaked. It slammed through Jamie's bedroom door. Jamie lived in the house. Jamie gave a sudden yell of help.

He woke up, he was having a nightmare. He got up sweating from the dream. He went downstairs to get a drink of water still sweating and breathing heavily from the dream. After finishing his drink of water, he went back upstairs and got back into his bed. After about five minutes he fell back to sleep. He had another one of his nightmares about the mysterious man who creeps into his house at night.

Once he woke from this nightmare, he screamed as the man from his dreams stood in his bedroom with a knife in his hand. Jamie screamed as loud as he could, but unfortunately no one was around the graveyard at night. The man came closer and stabbed Jamie. He died.

Dean Cooper (13)
The Grange School, Christchurch

The Game

The start of the whistle, the game had begun. Fans were chanting his name and cheering. He was amazed. Daniel wanted to play his heart out for his own fans who were cheering and waving, a full capacity crowd in the stadium.

There'd been an hour of the game with no goals, but suddenly, he had a strong feeling - something was going to happen.

Banners and flags with pictures on them and his name, he felt breathless and speechless. As he neared to the end of the pitch, the keeper was standing well out of the goal.

Goal!

He had lobbed the keeper. The stadium was set alight and they couldn't believe it.

Once the final whistle had blown, fans were on their feet, applauding Daniel for his fantastic performance. His team had won the Premiership for the very first time.

Daniel Cotterell (13)
The Grange School, Christchurch